Family Togetherness
Sophie MacDonald
Copyright Sophie MacDonald 2013
Published at Smashwords

This Is a Work of Fiction *involving an incest theme with consenting adults, and produced for adult entertainment only. If you do not agree with an adult incest theme do not read this story.*

All characters are over 18. All names, characters, places and incidents are used fictitiously. Any resemblance to actual events or locales or persons, living or dead, is entirely coincidental.

You MUST be over 18 years old to read this story. If you are under 18 or do not wish to view adult content, you must exit now. *Adults Only.*

Share your thoughts with us.
Take a moment to tell us how we're doing. Your feedback really matters.

You can reach us by:
Email: ***my777books@yahoo.com***

Search for other titles by **Sophie MacDonald.**

Family Togetherness

CHAPTER 1

It was the middle of a long hot summer the year I turned 18 that it started. There are only three of us in our family, Marie, my mother, and Debbie my sister. I'm Wayne. Debbie and I are fraternal twins. We never knew our father, he took off when he found out our mother was pregnant. We don't miss him, this however caused all sorts of problems with our grandparents, they were very religious and disowned mom. Luckily her grandmother took her in and looked after her. Because of this mom was able to complete high school and college. Now mom has a great job; she works for a large company. Her job was to go into new companies that they bought and integrate them with the rest of the group. She was very good at her job, and well paid, with great bonuses. The only downside was that we were usually only in one place for a few months, then it's on to the next. All this moving has bound us closer together because we knew we couldn't afford to get to involved with new people. Since the company was moving us they paid for our accommodation that meant that mom was able to save a lot of her pay. So when mom finally took a permanent job she was able to buy a great house. It's two stories, on a large fully fenced section, with a swimming pool. Because of the hot weather we have virtually all the time, (it seems like its sunny 52 weeks of the year) the windows are tinted to cut down on sun damage.

Anyway, Debbie was away for the week, on a school trip. It was the early hours of

Saturday morning when I was woken suddenly by rain pounding against the window by my head. When I realised what had woken me I decided I'd better check that all the windows were shut. I checked the windows downstairs and found 2 of them open, luckily the rain was coming the other way, but I shut them anyway in case it changed direction. Once I'd finished I moved back upstairs to finish checking. When I came to my mothers' room I quietly opened the door.

Mom was still asleep, I wasn't surprised. Mom works very hard during the week, and often has trouble getting to sleep with her thoughts churning away in her mind. So on Friday she usually takes a couple of strong sleeping pills so she can get to sleep easily and sleep through the night. Anyway I looked at the windows and they were shut. I was about to leave when I glanced at Mom again.

She looked so beautiful lying there. Her face, relaxed with sleep was even prettier than usual, her long blond hair spread over the pillow, her body outlined by the thin sheet that was covering her. I found myself drawn to her. "God, Wayne, she's your mother!" I thought. But even as I did, my cock started to harden. Now I get a lot of hard-ons, I guess its natural for a guy my age. To make it worse I was still a virgin, so my only release was with my own hand. The problem was that with all the moving around I'd never been in one place long enough to have a real girlfriend. Most school dances I'd taken Debbie because we were both unattached. In fact almost my only experience with the female body was from magazines and the Internet. Not really very satisfying. I suddenly realised that with Debbie gone I was alone in the house with a woman who could sleep through anything I did. If I played my cards right I might finally see a naked female body, even if it was my mothers. Having made up my mind to take the chance, I stepped quietly towards the bed, keeping an eye on mom, just in case.

Moving to the side of the bed, I took the sheet in my fingers and gently started pulling it down to expose my mothers' body. I stopped when I reached her breasts. Her nightie was transparent; I could see her breasts clearly through it. They were beautiful, rosy tipped mounds, I couldn't resist, and I just had to touch them. Keeping an eye on her face I reached out moved my hand inside the top of her nightie and covered her breast with my hand. It was unbelievable, I was finally touching a naked breast, and it was my mothers! Gently I started to run my hand over her breast, and, emboldened by her lack of reaction I covered her other breast with my other hand. There I was cupping my mothers' breasts, playing with them. I had touched a few breasts before; it was about as far as I had time to get with my various girlfriends before moving, but always through clothing. It was so much better naked, so much more exciting. Finally I pulled my hands away and returned them to the sheet, I had to see more, I had to make the most of this chance, who knew when I might get another, if ever. I eased the sheet down further, faster now, and more confident that she wouldn't wake. Finally I moved the sheet past her feet, she was wearing panties so I couldn't see her pussy, but I was so close. I pulled up her nightie leaving her covered only by her panties. It was a bit better, but the first thing I noticed was that I couldn't see much, she was lying on her back and her legs were together. All I could really see through her panties was her pubic hair. That at least answered one question, mom was a natural blond. I'd often wondered since Debbie and I are dark haired, and I know my pubic hair is dark as well, I guess we get that from our father. I reached down stroking over her pubic hair, feeling it crinkle through the thin material.

Oh well, I'd come so far I might as well go all the way. I grasped the waistband of moms panties and carefully worked them past her hips and then pulled them all the way off. Then I gently moved moms' legs apart exposing her genitals to my view. I could clearly see her pussy; her pubic hair was more of a frame than an obstacle. I was surprised to see it wasn't like most of the pussies I'd seen in magazines; there were no prominent labia. It was a tight-lipped, well defined slit, it looked beautiful. I had to know what it felt like

As my fingers touched her pussy lips mom moved! I froze, then realised she was opening her legs slightly, she was reacting to my touch, but she was still asleep. I ran my fingers up and down her slit, her legs opening wider and wider in response to my stimulation. Carefully I climbed onto the bed, moving between my mothers now widely spread legs. Then, once I was in position I leaned forward to look even closer at my mothers most private parts, the parts a son should never see, the parts a son should never think of his mother even having.

I was finally seeing a pussy for the first time, a real pussy not a picture of one. And the fact that it was my mothers seemed to make it even more exciting and more of a turn on. I leaned forward, even closer as I reached out to touch her again. I gently opened the lips of her vulva, the first thing I noticed was the moisture, she was wet! My mothers sleeping body was becoming sexually excited. I was turning my mother on! I could see everything, her clit was quite prominent, and most of all the entrance to her vagina. It was hard to believe that I had come out of such a small hole. Then I realised that something else was hard also, very hard. My cock was now fully erect inside my pajama pants. I had to get relief, and soon! I was about to go back to my room and masturbate, again, when I suddenly realised that mom was in the perfect position. I could run my cock up and down her pussy and come in a face cloth. Great idea! I carefully got off the bed and went to the bathroom and grabbed one, returning quickly to my previous position.

Holding the cloth in one hand I moved forward so my cock was only about an inch away from my target. I hesitated, and thought about what I was about to do. Here I am on my mothers' bed, kneeling between my sleeping mothers legs, about to touch her pussy with my cock. Did I really want to do this? Hell yes!

Finally decided I moved my cock forward that last inch, contact! My cock was touching pussy lips for the first time, and they were my own mothers' pussy lips. I gently began to stroke my cock up and down her slit. It was an amazing feeling. My cock was touching my mothers' pussy, the pussy I had been born out of, the pussy my father had penetrated and shot his sperm into, the sperm that had become Debbie and me. I stroked moms stomach, I had grown inside here I thought, before entering the world from between my mothers legs. Just like I was entering another new world between her legs today. Then I thought, why just touch her pussy? This is my chance to feel what its like to have my cock in a pussy, if only I had the guts. Suddenly I was burning with excitement, I had to do it. I had to put my cock inside my mother. I decided I'd put it in carefully and leave it there for a while before pulling out again.

Reaching down I again splayed her pussy lips, then with my other hand I guided my cock to that little, but oh so important, hole between her legs. I lined my cock up so that the head was positioned correctly, and slowly pushed forward. As I watched my cockhead slowly entered my mothers' vagina, it was tight but I was moving in. It was unbelievably exciting, seeing my cock penetrating a woman for the first time, and not just any woman, my mother. Then the head was in, I was in, I was inside my first woman, and she was, after all I had been here before, I was coming home. It felt so warm and snug, so welcoming, it was as if I belonged here, as if this special place was made for me, and me alone. I continued easing my cock into her; it seemed to take forever, even though I am only just over 6 inches long. Finally all my cock was in her, I was balls deep in my mothers pussy. I froze, letting the sensations run through me, her vaginal muscles contracting on my shaft, it was a wonderful feeling. It was just a shame that this would be my only chance to have it; I knew I wouldn't have the courage to try again. I wouldn't want to take the chance of being caught. Then mom started to move, my god, was she waking up? What would she say if she woke and found her son buried in her pussy up to his balls? I needn't have worried; she settled down again, it'd been close.

Then, suddenly, before I was ready to pull out, I started to come. My cock was fulfilling its purpose, it was delivering my sperm deep inside a female, it didn't know it was shooting my cum into my mother, but I did, and I loved it! I held myself still as I shot my sperm into my mothers' womb, into the womb my sister and I had been created in, I was really coming home. Finally the spasms eased and, its job done, my cock started to soften and slowly came out of moms' pussy. I reached forward with the cloth to wipe up my cum, but there was very little to wipe. I was relieved I hadn't made a mess on the bed.

Carefully I pulled up her panties, it was a lot harder getting them on than taking them off. Then I replaced the sheet, reluctantly covering her beautiful body. I bent down and kissed her softly on the lips before heading back to bed. I lay there for a while thinking about what had happened, I realised I still hadn't made love with a woman, what I'd really done was use moms body to masturbate with, but at least I'd finally been inside a woman. God, I thought as I dozed off, I'd really loved being inside my mother.

Next morning I was up making breakfast when I heard the shower start upstairs. Mom had finally woken up. In my minds eye I could see the water running down her naked body, I was starting to become aroused. Shaking myself I went back to preparing breakfast. It was on the table when mom came in the door dressed in her bathrobe. "Morning, Mom." I said when I saw her. She didn't say a word; she just walked up to me.

"Wayne, what happened last night?" she asked.

"Nothing," I replied, "we had a bit of a storm but there was no damage."

"If nothing happened what's this?" she said as she held up one of her fingers.

There on her fingertip was a drop of cum, damn, I thought, how did I miss that? I was sure I'd cleaned up carefully. "Well, go on, I know its cum, I just want to know how it got on my leg. Last time I looked you're the only male in the house."

I panicked, and started babbling. "I'm sorry mom. I came into your room while I was checking the windows, and I peeked at you under the sheet. While I was doing that I came, I guess some of it landed on you."

Mom just looked at me, shaking her head. "Wayne, Wayne, Wayne, you might as well tell me the whole truth. I didn't really find the cum on my leg, it came out of my pussy when I stood up. Did you fuck me in my sleep?"

I gave up. "No mom, not really, I only put my cock in you once and left it there, I meant to withdraw before I came, but I got too excited."

Mom just smiled, "There, that wasn't so hard was it?"

"You're not angry?" I asked in bewilderment.

"No, you're just a horny teenager who took advantage of the situation. I kind of wish I'd known so I could have enjoyed it too. Until last night I haven't had a real cock in me since your father left."

I suddenly realised that the same circumstances that had keep me a virgin had also stopped her having sex. She must be really horny I thought. Then I realised, maybe she was horny enough. "Mom," I said hesitatingly. She looked up. "We could try it again, if you like."

Her eyes widened as she realised what I was suggesting, then she smiled and said, as she moved to the door, "Race you to the bedroom."

As I followed her up the stairs she dropped her robe as she ran, and continued stark naked into her room. She was standing by the bed when I entered the room, my eyes roamed over her body now totally exposed in broad daylight, she was even more beautiful than last night. As I started toward her she held up a hand and said, "No. First I want to see you, take off those clothes." Since I was only wearing shorts and a tee shirt it didn't take me long to undress. It felt strange, standing there, naked, in front of my mother as she ran her eyes up and down my body. "Wayne you certainly have grown up haven't you, you're not my little boy any more. I think I'm going to enjoy this as much as you." With that she held out her arms and I walked into them, our lips met in our first kiss as lovers, as our bodies met I felt her breasts against my chest, and my cock against her stomach. "God, I'm so ready, lets just do it, I can't wait."

We fell together onto the bed, and as we rolled around mom positioned herself on her back, and, as she opened her legs and raised her knees, she guided me between them. Reaching down she grasped my cock and guided it to her pussy. As she felt the head enter her vagina she gasped, "Now, Wayne, now." With that I drove forward, watching moms eyes as she felt me penetrate her, she was so wet. "Fuck me, Wayne, fuck me hard."

I began to do just that, I began thrusting in and pulling back, varying the speed and depth of my penetration. A couple of times I pulled back too far and slipped out, I quickly guided myself back in. My lips found hers and they crushed together in a wild passionate kiss, my tongue entering her mouth even as my cock entered her vagina. Suddenly she gasped, and shuddered, her vaginal muscles contracting on my cock. She was coming! I'd made my mother come! I slowed down, waiting for her to come down from her high. She opened her eyes and smiled up at me, then her eyes widened as she realised I hadn't come yet. Mom hooked her legs around mine, cradling me with her body. "Come in me Wayne, I want your cum in me, I want your cum."

I drove into her again, and again, and again. Gaining speed as I drove myself to my own orgasm. As I drove in she eagerly raised her hips to meet me, taking me even deeper into her body. Our wild dance continued until, finally I could feel myself beginning to come. I drove as deep into my mother as I could and froze. Realising what was happening she clasped me to her tightly, gasping out, "Give it to me, give me your cum." At that point I couldn't have stopped doing it if had wanted to, and I didn't. I could feel my cock shooting shot after shot of my cum deep into my mothers womb for the second time that day. Only this time was so much better that last. This time I was really fucking my mother, and this time she knew what was happening and was fucking me back. It was wonderful.

But all good things must come to an end, and, finally, I was done. I had fulfilled the basic instinct of any male, to mate with a female and deposit my sperm into my partner. Still keeping my cock inside her, I rolled onto my side, bringing my mother with me. We lay there still joined, kissing, as we came down from our high. After a few minutes, mom looked deeply into my eyes, "That was wonderful Wayne. It's been so long for me. I hope you're not sorry we did this, I know I'm not."

I just smiled, "I'm not sorry at all. I loved it, I want to do it again and again."

Mom laughed, looking down at my cock that had finally slipped out of her vagina. "I think we had better wait awhile, I think my new toy here needs a rest. And right now I need another shower." Moving to the side of the bed mom got up and started heading to the bathroom, I watched her all the way. Just before she got to the door she laughed and turned to face me. "Now you can see how I found out." She said, pointing at her crotch. I laughed as I saw a stream of my cum flowing down her leg. Mom looked up at me. "I don't know why you're laughing, I really didn't want to waste that load, I wanted to keep it in me for a while."

"Go and get your shower mom, I guess I'll have to see about replacing it, later."

Mom smiled, "You are such a good son, being so kind to your mother." Then she turned, entered the bathroom and shut the door behind her. I sighed; wishing I could be in that shower with her, but I knew it would be a while before I was ready again. So I got out of bed, picked up my clothes and went and had a shower in my room. As I washed my cock I thought to myself, "Later, later."

CHAPTER 2

As soon as I finished my shower I left the house, I wanted to avoid any temptation until I was ready to act on it. I didn't really go anywhere; I just drove around thinking about what had happened that morning. I just couldn't believe that I'd just had sex, real sex, for the first time, and with my mother! Eventually I decided it was time to go back home and see what might develop next.

When I arrived home I put the car away and went in the house looking for mom. I searched the house but she wasn't there. I started to get worried, what if she was feeling guilty, what if she'd left. Then I glanced out the window and saw she was in the backyard, sunbathing. I immediately relaxed and headed out back. When I got out there I saw to my surprise that she was sunbathing nude. Now the yard was, as I said earlier, surrounded with a high fence and there are no nearby houses over looking it, but still I hadn't expected anything like this. I just stood there looking at her.

She looked so beautiful, glistening with suntan oil; her golden hair almost seemed to be glinting in the sun. I ran my eyes over her naked body, growing more excited by the moment. Finally I'd had enough. I walked over to her and placed my hand on her shoulder. Mom opened her eyes and smiled up at me. "I'm glad you're back Wayne. I was beginning to worry. I thought you might have been sorry about what we did."

I reached down and started caressing one of her breasts, "Sorry? Hell no! I'm glad it happened. I couldn't be happier." As I bent down to kiss her I felt her nipple harden against the palm of my hand, she was becoming turned on again.

"Well Wayne, what would you like to do next?" she asked when our lips finally separated.

"Could I, could I have a look at your body, a real look? If you don't mind, I mean."

"God, Wayne. I've had sex with you, letting you look at me is nothing in comparison." She replied in exasperation. "Lets go inside and get this show and tell underway." Standing, she led the way into the house, I followed, watching her all the way, watching the movement of the muscles of her thighs and butt as she led me into the living room, she looked as beautiful going as coming. There she turned to face me. "Okay Wayne, start looking." I was. Her body had a nice golden tan which I suddenly realised had no tan lines, she obviously always sunbathed nude. Damn, how many times had I missed the opportunity to peek at her, not that it mattered now. Still it was frustrating. While I was staring at her I realised she had started talking. I forced myself to concentrate on what she was saying.

"Okay, Wayne. From now on, if you follow my rules, whenever we can, my body belongs to you, well almost all of it. Let me guide you around your new property. First my breasts." She said. Reaching up and cupping them in her hands. "Now, they are not very big, I'm only 32b, but I think they're a nice handful." I just nodded, watching her hands caress her breasts. "As you can see, when I'm excited my nipples are about an half inch long. I love having them sucked. I always have. In fact, I used to get so hot breastfeeding you and Debbie, that I usually had to masturbate afterwards. Now lets move on to the main event, my pussy." With that Mom moved over to a chair, sat down, put her feet up on the coffee table, and slowly, teasingly, moved them apart, exposing her pussy to me.

"First, this is my pussy, you can call it that, it's real name, at least for what you can see now is the vulva, you can even call it that if you want. What you can't call it if, you want me to let you into it, is the 'c' word. I hate that word and always have. You understand?" Seeing my nod she continued. "Good. Now these are my pussy lips or labia. During foreplay I like to have them caressed lightly. Like this." Gently she began running her fingers up and down the lips, lightly stroking them. She continued doing it for a few minutes, as I gazed entranced at my mother pleasuring herself. Finally I noticed a slight sheen of moisture coating the lips, and that they were starting to part. She was really turned on.

Taking a deep breath she continued. "Now I'll show you the rest." Reaching down she separated the labia. "Here is the entrance to my vagina," she said, pointing to the hole I'd already been in twice. " as you know from this morning. But this is," she said, moving her finger up, "for women more important. My clitoris. I often need direct stimulation here to make me come. Though, I must admit you did a pretty good job last time without touching it. I was so hot, so turned on, so excited to be having sex again. And with my son! God, I really loved it."

"Me too, mom, me too."

"Now before we go on I want to make one final thing clear. We can make love whenever its safe, my pussy belongs to you, you can do what you like with it. I'll let you do whatever you want, except one thing. I'm not into anal sex; you can use my mouth and my pussy all you want. But that's it. If you try to use my ass I'll cut you off, totally. That's my only condition, do you accept it?"

"Yes, mom, I agree. I won't touch your ass."

"I didn't say you couldn't touch it," she laughed, "you just can't stick your cock in it. But I think you'll be happy where you can stick it. I know I will. In fact," she said, "I missed breakfast this morning, and I don't suppose you could get me a snack to tide me over until lunch."

"Sure," I said, "how about a sandwich?"

"No, I don't think so, how about your cock? I haven't eaten you yet, and I love the taste of cum."

Stepping forward, I dropped my pants and shorts, exposing my fully erect organ. "Bon Appetite, Mom."

Mom smiled, and leaned forward, "Mmm, this looks finger licking good." She reached out cupping my balls in one hand, lightly bouncing them. "Nice. I think I'm going to get a good meal this morning." Then she took my cock in her other hand and guided it to her lips. She was done talking.

She began by running the head of my cock back and forth along her lips, and then she extended her tongue and commenced moving it around the head, lapping up the pre cum that was already forming. Finally, she opened her mouth just enough, and moved her head forward, enveloping my cock. Once the first 2 inches were inside her mouth she started stroking my cock with her tongue again. God, it felt great. I moved my hands to her head and held it in place. Mom looked up at me, she smiled, or at least as much as she could around my cock.

Finally she stopped using her tongue. She pulled her head back a little then pushed forward, a little further than before. Mom quickly got into a rhythm, her strokes were not very large, and she usually gained only about half an inch at a time. But, before long she was taking my entire organ in her mouth, and she was clearly enjoying it as much as I was. Then, all of a sudden she pulled back completely and my cock fell from between her lips. Before I could say anything she held my cock up and began running her tongue up and down the shaft. Then she started lapping at my balls, running her tongue all over my scrotum, she opened her mouth and took my scrotum into her mouth, one ball at a time. Now she was flexing her cheeks as well as using her tongue. My balls were being directly stimulated, really stimulated, too stimulated. I had to warn her I was about to come.

When I told her, mom quickly swallowed my cock again, and started bobbing her head like there was no tomorrow. Finally it was time, all I could do was gasp, "Now, mom, now." As my cum started surging up my shaft. Realising it was time mom pulled back on my cock until only the head was still in her mouth, and she rapidly flickered her tongue over the head as my cum started shooting into her mouth. Shot after shot entered her mouth, she swallowed as fast as she could, but some spilled out of her mouth onto her face, it was an amazing sight, my mother, my cock in her mouth, her throat moving as she swallowed the sperm that I was shooting into her mouth, streaks of cum coating her chin. Finally it was over, mom gently cleaned off the head of my cock before pulling back and letting it drop free. Reaching up, she wiped up the stray cum with her fingers, and then licked them clean. Once she finished she smiled at me, "Thanks, Wayne, that was delicious."

"I'm glad you liked it Mom," I replied. "Sit on the edge of the sofa, I want to return the favour."

After she sat down I knelt in front of her, picked up her legs and placed them over my shoulders, fully exposing her crotch to me. With the position of her legs and her excitement, the lips of her slit were starting to gape, prepared for penetration. Not this time I thought. I leant forward and ran my tongue up and down her pussy. Over the soft lips and into the split between. Mom gasped at the contact, reached out, and held my head in place, as I had with her. I continued my assault lapping up moms' juices as they flowed out.

Then, opening her labia fully, I drove my tongue into her vagina, circling the entrance, faster and faster. By now mom was really getting into it, moaning to beat the band. I was proud I was doing a good job, but I could see she needed something more to push her over the edge. Remembering what she'd said about her clitoris I moved to the top of her pussy, and took her now very prominent clit in my mouth. Once I was ready I started sucking hard on her clit, while caressing it with quick, flickering strokes of my tongue. Mom gasped again as her orgasm hit. I slowed down my action as she came, but kept up some stimulation until she pushed my head away from between her legs. I moved up on the sofa with her, taking her in my arms lightly stroking her back, and softly kissing her, as she came down from her high.

"Mom," I said finally.

"Yes, Wayne?"

"Did you mean it when you said that your pussy belongs to me?"

"Of course I did, so long as you follow my rule about anal sex, and you're careful when other people are around." She replied.

"Great. Well here is my only rule; from now on you are not allowed to wear panties, except during your period. I want to be able to access your pussy at any time I want, even if it's just a touch."

"If that's what you want, consider it done. I have officially stopped wearing panties from this minute. What do you want to do now?" she asked, reaching down and stroking my cock.

"Lets have eat, we'll go to the movies tonight after dinner."

Mom was obviously surprised with my choice, "Are you sure?"

"I certainly am, I want to go on a date with my new girlfriend."

CHAPTER 3

Finally we were on the way to the movies, the tension had been high during lunch and dinner, mom kept watching me, waiting for me to do something. I wanted to, I really did. But I'd decided it would be better if I just let the anticipation grow. It was only a short drive to the cinema. As I drove, I put my right arm around mom and pulled her against me. Mom rested her head on my shoulder as my hand cupped her breast through her clothes, I gently manipulated it as I drove, her nipple bored into my palm the whole way. When we got there we decided to see the new Meg Ryan romantic comedy. I didn't care what we saw; I just wanted to get in there. We took seats in the back, because it was such a lovely evening, and because the film was really a date movie, the theatre filled up quickly. It was perfect; I'd been counting on it. When the film finally started, I carefully covered our laps with my jacket. I was ready to begin.

I moved my hand under cover onto moms' thigh. She quickly glanced at me, obviously realising what I was about to do, I leaned over and whispered to her. "Open your legs, I want to check you're following my rule." Mom just smiled and nodded. Then I felt her legs begin to spread apart as she followed my instruction. When she stopped moving I started to slowly run my hand up and down her thigh, teasing her, edging closer and closer to my target. Finally my fingers hit pay dirt, they touched her bare pussy. Mom wasn't wearing any panties! She meant what she'd said; she was mine to do with as I would. I was in heaven. Unlimited potential opened up before me. But for now I decided to just enjoy the moment. It was so sexy, a mother, not wearing her panties, sitting in a dark movie theatre with her son, surrounded by people, letting him touch her pussy. God, I wanted to fuck her right then and there, unfortunately that was impossible. Still I could have a lot of fun with her.

I gently started to rub my finger up and down her slit, feeling her moisture slowly starting to flow. Then I pulled my damp fingers out from under the jacket, and while she watched I licked them clean, tasting her juices. Once I was finished I reached back into her crotch and started again. This time I applied a little more pressure and pushed my finger past her labia, I circled her hole a few times, then drove my finger into her, and stopped. It was unbelievable; there I was, sitting with my mother in a public place, with my finger buried to the knuckle in her pussy. I pulled my hand back until my finger was almost out and inserted a second finger. Then I slowly moved both fingers into her hot, tight, passage. I let my fingers just rest there for a few minutes, slightly flexing them, then slowly started to move them in and out, in and out, doing with my fingers what I wanted to do with my cock. After a while I paused again for a while before starting again. I kept this up for the remainder of the movie. Just keeping her stimulated, never bringing her off.

Finally the film finished, I pulled my fingers out, and quickly brought them to moms' mouth. I didn't say anything, I didn't have to. Mom took my fingers into her mouth where she quickly licked them clean. I stood and put my jacket on, when mom got up and turned to lead the way out I noticed an wet patch on the back of her dress, she'd really been turned on. I looked down at her seat, and, sure enough, there was a dark patch where her crotch had been. I stopped mom. "Look at the seat." I told her. Mom looked, she blushed when she realised what had happened. Then she gasped, mom quickly looked around to see if anyone was watching her, then she touched the back of her dress. It didn't take her long to find the wet patch. "Wayne, is it very obvious?" I just nodded. "Could you give me your jacket?"

"No, mom, I like you the way you are, your dress looks beautiful. Lets go to the car." I led mom slowly out of the theatre, my arm around her, my hand resting on her hip, hopefully drawing attention to the wet patch. I wanted people to see it, to realise what it was, to guess what I'd been doing. As we neared the entrance we passed a mirror, I looked and sure enough 5 or 6 people were stareing at moms' dress, smiling. I whispered into her ear, "Look in the mirror." I felt her tense as she looked and realised the patch had been noticed, she didn't say a word, she just kept walking.

Once we were outsid on the way back to the car mom whispered in my ear, "God, Wayne, I'm so hot, all those people know I was letting you play with my pussy. I could jump you right here and now."

"Sorry, mom. You've got to wait until we get home. You drive this time. When we get to the car pull up your dress so I can see your pussy while you drive."

Once we got in the car mom did exactly what I asked. It was wild, driving down through town, my mothers pussy in clear view, even if, because of our tinted windows the only one who could see it was me. I watched as her labia (which were already swollen and parted with arousal) slightly opened and closed as mom used the pedals. The scent of her arousal filled the air. Mom was really on fire.

When we got home mom quickly led the way into the house. Once the door was closed behind us she threw herself into my arms, covering my face with kisses as she ground her lower body into mine. Pulling away she gasped, "Come on, I've got to have it, now!" She turned towards the stairs, but I stopped her in her tracks.

"No, mom. I can't wait for us to get to your room. We'll do it right here."

Mom didn't argue, she simply lay down, lifted her dress, and opened her legs; she was really ready for it. I stood there looking down at my horny mother and slowly started to remove my clothes. Her eyes followed every move until I finally pulled down my shorts and my cock sprang free. Mom moaned as she gazed up at my organ, then she simply held up her arms to me. I came forward, but instead of moving into place between her thighs, I grabbed one of her hands and pulled her to her feet. Quickly turning her around and pushing her down to her hands and knees. Then I flipped up her dress, exposing her ass. She was in the classic doggy position. Looking over her shoulder she just said, "Remember my rule." I remembered, but that was okay. There was only one place I wanted to be. I moved into position behind her on my knees, and then guided my cock up and down her slit, teasing her, and me. Mom started pushing back, trying to trap my cock. Finally I was ready. I lined myself up and drove into her all the way in one long stroke. Mom threw back here head, "Yes! Yes! God, yes!" she screamed. I reached around to grab her breasts as I began to fuck her slowly and steadily. Mom was meeting my thrusts with thrusts of her own as I continued to drive deep into her. I had gotten her so hot she was no longer thinking with her head. Her pussy was in total control of her body, it only wanted one thing and it was getting it.

I started squeezing her breasts as I increased my pace, then I stopped moving altogether, but mom didn't, she kept moving, forward and back, fucking herself on my cock. It was almost time, I started stroking into her again, and then I leaned forward and whispered to her "I'm coming mom, I'm coming." She redoubled her efforts, determined to come as well. Soon I felt my semen welling up from my balls, then, just before my cock started to shoot my load into my mother, I drove as deep as I could and held myself in place. I exploded; spurt after spurt of cum was shot deep inside moms' vagina. I reached down and gently squeezed her clit, triggering her own orgasm. Her vaginal walls squeezing my cock harder, trying to force more cum into her.

Finally our mutual orgasms subsided. We were both totally drained. I slumped over moms' back,she turned her head and kissed me. "That was wonderful, I've never cum so hard before."

"Neither have I, mom, neither have I." Was all I could say.

After a while I pulled my softening cock out of moms' pussy, we stood up and started to go upstairs. Part way up I told mom to take her dress off. She didn't hesitate an instant, mom undid the buttons and pulled her dress over her head, she stood there naked except for her bra, as I ran my eyes over her body. I could see the traces of our lovemaking coating the lips of her pussy, I loved it, I loved having my mother displaying her body to me. I wanted more, I simply said, "Take off your bra." Mom reached behind her and undid her bra, quickly removing it. Mom continued up the stairs stark naked, it was almost as if she revelled in being controlled. If that were the case I would make the most of it.

When we got to the top of the stairs, I told her that she wasn't to take a shower or wear any clothes for the rest of the evening, I wanted to be able to see my cum running out of her pussy. So from now on she wasn't allowed to wipe up any of my sperm that trickled out of her until she got my permission to do so, then, so it wouldn't go to waste, she was to eat it.

The rest of the evening was a surreal experience. My mother was totally naked the whole time, while I was fully dressed. She made us a late supper naked, ate it naked, she was naked when we did the dishes. When we watched TV I had her sit with her legs spread wide so when I looked her way, which was quite often, I could see her pussy. And all through this time, every now and then, my cum seeped out of her slit. It was a real turn on to see my cum emerging from my mothers pussy, and dribbling down her thighs. Then, every time she'd ask me, "Wayne, can I eat your cum?" I'd usually wait until it had run some way down her thigh before giving permission. And then she'd scoop up each drop and suck it off her finger. Mom was obviously totally into being controlled sexually by her son. And I wasn't going to complain.

Finally it was time for bed, I told mom to take a shower. I was waiting in bed for her when she returned; she dropped her robe and joined me. We made love, much slower this time. When we came I rolled to the side, moms legs still holding me deep inside her. As we drifted off to sleep our arms around each other, I thought about tomorrow. Tomorrow I'd have more fun with mom, tomorrow we'd be going to church.

CHAPTER 4

When I woke next morning, for a second, I was confused about where I was it wasn't my room. Then I remembered, smiling I turned to mom, she was still asleep. Pulling back the sheet I looked at her naked body, the body I'd grown so used to in such a short time, barely over 24 hours. I could see traces of my cum from our last session on her thighs and pubic hair, I leaned over and kissed each breast, and then woke her with a kiss on her mouth. "Morning, mom."

"Morning, Wayne."

"Before we go to church we'd better clean the house a little." I said. Climbing out I reached down and pulled mom from bed. "No clothes. Either of us."

Mom just smiled and went into the toilet. After she returned we headed downstairs. There wasn't really very much to do, have breakfast, and a little straightening. But those chores are so much more fun when you're not wearing clothes. The chores took a little longer than they should have. We were both looking at the other. Any job takes on a new meaning when you do it naked I guess. Finally we were finished. It was time to move onto the next stage of my plan. I took moms hand and led her upstairs. We didn't go to bed as she obviously expected, (she could quite clearly see my erect cock leading the way) instead we went into the bathroom and I started the shower. Fortunately it is a large shower. Once the water reached the correct temperature I led mom into the stall.

As the water cascaded over us I started to wash her. First I'd soap up the cloth and then gently run it over her body, stroking her, caressing her. I washed her entire body, except for her pussy; I was saving that for last. When it was finally time to wash it, I soaped up my hand instead. As I washed her pussy with my bare hand I told her I'd want to shave her pubic hair later. Mom just grinned. Then it was her turn to wash me; she did the same as I had done. The feel of her hand washing my cock and balls was wonderful. I decided then and there that from now on, whenever we could, this would be the way we'd shower in future, having someone else wash you is so much better.

Once the last of the soapsuds were washed away I moved forward, pushing mom up against the wall, kissing her, hard. Her arms tightened around me as our bodies crushed together, and the water played over us. I reached down and started to caress the pussy that I'd become so familiar with, mom reached for my cock. We kissed harder. Then I splayed the lips of her slit open, and crouched slightly. Mom, realising what I intended guided my cock into her pussy. When I felt the head safely enclosed in the entrance to her vagina, I slowly eased in, pushing mom up against the wall as I did so. Once I had fully penetrated her, I cupped her buttocks and lifted her. Mom automatically wrapped her legs behind my butt. We adjusted ourselves slightly until we were both comfortable. Then I began to fuck her. As I drove in and out of her body, I moved her forward and backward with my hands. "Harder, Wayne, faster, I want it all." She gasped in my ear. I obliged as she covered my face with kisses. It seemed to go on and on, but it really was probably only three or four minutes before I shot my cum. Once more my mothers vagina and womb were filled with her sons seed. I quickly lowered her to the floor and turned off the shower. We just stood there, heads on each others shoulders, totally fulfilled.

I realised that we didn't have much time left. I dragged mom out of the shower and we quickly dried each other. "Come on, we have to get ready for church." I told her. "Today you will wear no underwear at all." Mom just nodded, she went to her closet, picked out a dress and put it on over her naked body. "You know this is not right, going to church without any underwear, with my sons sperm in my belly." I could tell she wasn't really concerned, in fact she seemed turned on with the thought, so I just told her that from now on I'd be the one that would say what was right or wrong for us.

To make sure she didn't make a mess on her way out I had her cup her hand over her pussy, holding it closed, so my cum wouldn't escape. Then, in the car, I pulled her dress up so, if there were any leakage, it wouldn't mark her dress, and, not wanting to mark the seat I replaced her hand with mine. We drove with my hand fully planted between her legs, covering her pussy. When we arrived, at the last minute before we got out, I removed my hand and pulled down her dress.

In church all I could think of was my mother, my lover, sitting next to me listening to the sermon, naked under her dress, with my cum trickling out of her pussy. I was hard the whole time. It got even worse when mom stopped to talk to the minister as we were about to leave. From where I was standing I noticed a small glob of semen slowly run down her thigh. She looked as if butter wouldn't melt in her mouth. Once she was finished talking I rushed her to the car, I wanted to get home, fast. Mom, however wasn't in a hurry, "I felt really depraved when I was talking to the minister. I was thinking if only he knew I was fucking my son. Then I felt your cum on my leg, God it was exciting, knowing if anyone looked they could see that I'd just had sex. Even if they didn't know whose sperm was running down my leg."

When we got home I jumped mom as soon as the door closed, again I fucked her in the hall. This time as I drove into mom I could feel the remnants of our previous coupling; I could feel the sperm my cock was displacing coating my cock and balls, and her pussy lips. It was enough to drive me over the edge quite quickly, adding a new load to her pussy. Once we came down from our high, mom said that it had been great, but that she was worried about how much time we'd have together after Debbie came home next weekend. I told her not to worry, so long as we were careful we'd have plenty of opportunities to be together. By now I was starting to become erect again, it's hard not to when you're holding your naked mother in your arms. Mom just laughed when she felt my organ prodding her belly. "Looks like Wayne is ready for a little more fun with his mother, I know I am."

Standing mom grasped my cock and led me by it into the kitchen. There she sat me down on a chair and fell to her knees in front of me. "Lets just get this nice and ready for me." She said. She took my cock into her mouth, gently sucking and lubricating it. When she was satisfied, she stood, and, holding my cock erect guided it into her pussy as she lowered herself onto it. Once my cock was fully seated in her vagina she slowly started to ride me, all I could really do was sit there as she set the pace. It was the first time I'd been able to watch my cock entering my mother the sight blew my mind. The feeling of my cock driving into her already cum filled pussy was wonderful, we'd never done it twice so close together before, I reached down to stimulate her clit so she would be able to come as well. And it was her climax that triggered mine, the muscles of her vagina contracted on my cock, once again I came in my woman, and that was what she really was, mine. The fact that she was also my mother didn't matter. I was just a male, mating with his female.

We sat there, still joined for several minutes. Then, looking at me, mom said, "I'm really full, I better be careful or I could make a mess."

Realising what she meant I told her to get off me. She did, holding her hand over her pussy to keep my semen from running out of her. I went over and got a glass, then I placed it on the chair and positioned mom over it. I told her to take her hand away and let my cum run into the glass. Mom immediately did as I asked, after the initial flow of sperm mom opened her slit and concentrated on contracting her vaginal muscles to deposit more of my cum. By now I was on my knees, within inches of her pussy, watching everything, watching my cum trickle out of my mothers open vagina. When no more semen came out I picked up the glass, telling her that her snack was ready. Without the slightest hesitation mom took the glass and drank it straight down, she even licked around the sides of the glass to get the last few drops.

Leaving mom I went upstairs and got my shaving gear and a towel, it was time to shave moms' pubic hair. Getting back, I spread the towel on the kitchen counter and then helped her up onto it; I spread her legs and moved between them. First I dampened her curls, then applied the shaving foam, finally I was ready to begin. With short strokes I carefully removed the hair above her pussy. Then, holding her labia to the side, I shaved the left side of her pussy, and then the right. Finally I wiped up the few drops of foam that remained, it was done, moms' pussy was completely bare. "So, mom, what do you think?"

Mom bent forward to get a better look, "Well, it looks a little strange, I haven't been bare like this since I was shaved before I delivered you and your sister. The real question is what do you think?"

"I love it mom, your pussy looks so different without hair, and I think it looks even sexier than before. You'll have to be careful next time you sunbathe though, you don't want to be burned there."

"You're right about that Wayne. Wayne?"

"Yes, mom?"

"Do you think you could fuck me again now, just to see what it feels like, you know, as an experiment?"

Looking at my naked mother sitting there, with her shaved pubic mound, I decided that I'd like to take part in that experiment, very much. Taking moms hand we went upstairs to her room, no, on second thoughts I changed my mind, I guided mom into Debbies room, I wanted to take her in my sisters' bed. Mom didn't complain, she just went straight to the bed and, turning the covers down, climbed in and waited for me to follow. She didn't have long to wait.

I took mom in my arms and our bodies came together, I held her as we kissed, our mouths meeting in kiss after kiss, our tongues exploring each others mouths as we deepened our kissing. I began to run my hands over moms beautiful body. Pulling my mouth away from hers I dropped my head and took one of her nipples into my mouth, gently sucking on it as I caressed her other breast with my hand. Then I felt her hand reach for my rising cock, not wanting to be left behind I moved my hand into her crotch. Her pussy felt strange without the hair, strange but good. I could immediately feel that she was well lubricated, it was time. I rolled mom over onto her back and mounted her, holding her pussy open as she guided me in. I easily sank into her excited body, as mom hooked her legs around me. Once my cock was properly seated I began to slowly fuck my mother. Each time I drove into her depths my mother arched her hips wanting more, I gave her everything I had, wishing I was bigger so I could give her more. We established our now familiar rhythm; we were both now attuned to each others needs, and did everything we could to see they were met. I moved my mouth to moms ear, kissing her all the way. "How does it feel, mom, having sex in your daughters bed, with your son?"

Mom laughed, "It's great, it's such a turn on. Making love in your sisters bed, what will you think of next."

I was coming closer and closer to release until, finally, it was time. I drove into mom, harder and faster as the crisis approached. Mom slipped her hand between us and started to play with her clit. We both came together, my cum spurting, well, dribbling (after all it was the fourth time today) into her as she reached her orgasm.

Exhausted I dragged myself off of mom, slumping beside her, as my equally exhausted cock deflated.

After a while mom kissed me, "Thank you Wayne, that was just what I needed. So what did you think of my shaved pussy?"

I reached over and caressed her pussy, "It was wonderful, mom, I think it's great."

Mom looked down at my hand on her bare pussy, "I think it does too. I'll tell you one thing though, we're going to have to change Debbies sheets and air the room out, or she'll know something happened here."

Looking down I noticed the damp spot on the sheet and had to agree. I also realised that I would have to make the most of the time we had until Debbie returned. It was going to be a busy week, and I couldn't wait.

CHAPTER 5

It had been a wild week, mom and I had fucked like newlyweds the entire time I was home, I couldn't count the number of times I came in her. The time I was at school was wonderful too, I needed the rest, I must have been the calmest guy at school. I was having all the sex I wanted, anytime I wanted, the only trouble was I couldn't tell anyone about it, after all it was my mother I was sleeping with. Still all good things must come to an end, Debbie was coming back tomorrow, tonight was going to be our last night alone. I was determined to make it something special, to tide us over until our next opportunity. First I made us a nice candlelit dinner, and arranged soft music to play while we ate. I also had mom wear one of her nicest dresses, and, this time I told her to wear panties. The meal was lovely; we had a nice bottle of wine to go with it. We spent our time taking about various things, it was just like a real date, with the exception being that I knew I was going to get some later. Once we finished we decided to leave the dishes until tomorrow, and retired to the living room. I started the music and we danced, slowly, our bodies pressed against each other. Finally it was time.

We made our way to the couch, and into each others arms. We kissed, hard. When we finally separated all I could do was say, "What are we going to do when Deb comes back, we can't stop doing this. I love you too much to stop making love to you."

"And I love you too. Don't worry, we'll find a way." Mom said before she pulled me to her again.

This time while we kissed I took more direct action. I reached up and started to caress her breasts through her dress, I could feel her nipples rise in response; leaving one hand there I ran the other one up her leg under her dress. This time when my hand reached her crotch I encountered her panties, instead of the pussy I'd become so used to. In a way it was more erotic, caressing her pussy through those skimpy panties. It was like we were an ordinary couple making out. I slipped my fingers through the leg hole into her panties, when I made direct contact with her slit; it was obvious that she was as ready as I was. I worked a couple of fingers into her pussy, gently masturbating her as our kissing intensified. "Do it, Wayne, I want you in me, now!" mom gasped into my mouth. I released her breast, pulled my hand out of her panties, and moved both hands to the waistband, it was time to remove them.

I pulled her panties down her legs; not bothering to take them all the way off, leaving them hooked around one foot. Mom was equally busy, undoing my pants and pulling both them and my shorts down past my butt. I pushed mom back on the sofa, moving one leg so her foot rested on the floor, and raising the other up the back of the sofa. Then I moved into position between moms' thighs, and guided my organ to her entrance. With slow, steady pressure I drove my cock into my mothers depths. Mom gasped as I commenced to fuck her, raising her hips to receive me even deeper, as she hooked her legs around mine. We had established a nice rhythm when disaster struck. "Mom! Wayne! What are you doing?" it was Debbies voice. Moms' legs relaxed at once as I pulled out of her and turned to face the door. Sure enough Debbie was standing there. Obviously stunned by finding her mother and brother making love. "Deb, we can explain." I told her. All she said was that we had better.

Mom sat up next to me while I explained what had happened while she had been away, how mom and I had moved from a normal mother – son relationship, to something more. Mom told Debbie that she hadn't been forced to have sex with me, that when the opportunity presented itself she'd seized it with both hand. While mom was talking I had acted, automatically, without really realising it, perhaps seeking comfort, or to provide comfort. One of my hands was under moms dress, stroking her pussy. When Debbie noticed what I was doing she asked mom why she was letting me touch her like that. Mom laughed. "I'm letting him for three reasons, first, I like Wayne touching me like this. Second, he's very good at it. Third, when he first became my lover I told him that from then on my pussy belonged to him, he could do whatever he wanted with it. And he has, boy has he! I've enjoyed every minute of it."

It was obvious by now that Debbie had calmed down, and she wasn't going to run screaming from the house. What happened next however was a surprise. "Mom, I'm a virgin, I've never seen anything like what you and Wayne were doing. Could you start again, could you show me what its like to, you know, make love?"

Mom and I exchanged glances, when I saw her slight nod I stood, drawing her to her feet. "Come on Deb, lets go upstairs." I said as I started to lead mom from the room. Mom hesitated for a moment, and I glanced at her in time to see her kick her panties off the foot they were hooked around, then we continued. We didn't look back, but I could hear Debbie following us. This was going to be wild I thought, making love to my mother, while my twin sister watched. My cock twitched at the thought. And maybe after I'd finished with mom, who knows?

Once we got to the bedroom mom took over. She told Debbie to sit on a chair and then commenced her education into the art of lovemaking, the theory anyway. First, to get ready, she took off her dress and bra, standing naked in front of her daughter. Mom then said that she would show Deb what a naked man looked like and began stripping me. Once she was finished she stepped back to let Deb look all she wanted. I watched as Debbie ran her eyes up and down my body, obviously pausing to study my cock and balls. Her eyes widened, when, stimulated by having my sister studying my sexual equipment, my cock became fully erect, pointing at her. Debbie swallowed hard, and then blushed as she forced her eyes away. I looked at mom, and she smiled back and winked.

Now it was obviously time for the rest of the lesson, I was more than ready. Mom moved to the bed, lay down, and, after placing a pillow under her hips opened her legs for me. Boy was I ready. I went to the bed, feeling Debbie's eyes following me the whole way. Now it was time to show her what she had interrupted, what she wanted to see, her mother and brother making love. And I was only too pleased to oblige, in fact you might say it was my pleasure. Or rather, our pleasure, as both mom and I were obviously turned on by the thought of having an audience to our lovemaking. Especially with Debbie being the audience. As I moved up to mount my mother, I paused to lick the pussy I loved so much. Then I positioned myself for entry, whispering in moms ear, "Lets give Deb a real show."

Mom reached down and guided my cock into her vagina, it felt so much more exciting having Debbie there. Mom was so wet what with our previous activities and the situation, my cock slid into her with one easy motion. Once more we began the ageless dance of mating. Our lips locked together as I began surging backwards and forwards, seeking the depths of my mothers' vagina, driven by nature to plant my sperm as deep in my female as I could. Mom was equally driven, driven to take as much of my cum as she could. As I neared completion I reached down to stimulate moms' clit. The reaction was explosive. She threw her head back and cried out as she came. I drove deep and started spurting my cum into her. Finally we were done; I slumped down on mom, exhausted.

"That was wonderful, Mom, thanks for showing me." Debbie said. I started when I heard her voice; I'd gotten so involved I'd forgotten about our audience. I pulled out of mom and moved up to lie besides her looking at Deb. Debbie was standing at the foot of the bed, she had obviously moved closer to get a better view. She was looking at our bodies, we were quite a sight. A mother, her legs still widely spread, her obviously excited pussy, lips still slightly gaping, lying next to her son, his softening cock still wet with their mutual juices. "I never knew love making could be so beautiful. I don't blame you for having sex with each other. If I was in the same position I sure would," she said as she turned for the door.

"Debbie," Mom said, before she could reach the door, "would you like to see what its like? Would you like your brother to make love to you?"

Debbie paused, her hand on the doorknob, then slowly turned towards the bed. "Are you sure, mom?"

"I don't mind sharing your brother with you, and I bet Wayne won't mind either." All I could do was smile at the thought. When Deb realised this she smiled too. "Come on Debbie, take your clothes off, slowly, show your brother what he's getting. It'll help get him ready for you.

As Debbie started to undress, mom told her to leave her underwear for last. Deb slowly slipped off her blouse, (it wasn't a strip tease, it was better, it was a girl taking her clothes off for her lover) she paused standing there in skirt and bra, and then she reached down and unzipped her skirt, letting it fall to the floor. There she was in just her bra and panties, it was obvious, from the dark mark on the front of her panties that my sister was really turned on. Then it was time for her bra, she reached behind her back, unhooked it, and let it fall forward off her shoulders exposing her breasts. Finally, she hooked her fingers in the waist of her panties and quickly pulled them down and stepped out of them. I was finally looking at my sisters' naked body. She actually looked a lot like mom; her breasts were a little bigger.

Mom moved to the side, saying, "Come up here, Debbie, give your brother a kiss. After all he's going to be very nice to you soon."

Deb didn't hesitate, she moved into the space mom had just vacated, I took her in my arms and we kissed. Softly at first, then with greater passion, our bodies pressed together, and I felt my sisters' naked breasts pressing against my chest. It was crazy. Less than a week ago I'd been a virgin, now I'd just finished making love to my mother, and I was going to take my sisters virginity!

"Debbie," Mom interrupted, "before we go any further I think you should have a closer look at Waynes' body." Debbie blushed as she pulled away from me and moved down to look between my legs. "See Debbie? Look at his beautiful cock, it feels so good inside you. Look at his balls, go ahead touch him."

Debbie, hesitantly reached out and touched my cock, then more confident she took it in her hand, "It's so soft, I mean it's hard but it's soft." Debbie continued touching me, as she did so I was getting harder and harder. I wondered what Debbie was thinking about, there she was touching her brothers cock, the cock that was going to take her virginity, touching the balls that were going to produce the first cum her pussy was going to receive.

"Okay, Debbie, its time." Mom said, she had obviously taken over as master or should I say mistress of ceremonies. "Lay down here where I was." Debbie quickly did as asked. As she settled into position mom, who was now kneeling beside her, raised her legs so that her feet were flat on the bed, and then pushed my sisters' legs apart, exposing her pussy. Debbie blushed when she saw how exposed she was, she tried to close her legs, but mom kept them open. "It's OK darling, don't worry, you're going to love your brother making love to you. You'll love having him look at your body, I know I do." Looking down, she said, "She's not quite ready, I think you'd better help."

Only too pleased I knelt between my sisters' legs, my cock only inches from its target. For the first time I really looked at her pussy. It was as beautiful as moms, nice tight lips, a perfect slit between her thighs. I reached out to touch it, to touch her soft, satiny skin. A shudder ran through her body as she felt the first male hand touch her most intimate place. A place that only she and her gynaecologist (who was also a female) had touched before. I began to stimulate her, using the skills and techniques I'd learned with mom, they worked as well with Deb. She became more relaxed, and her pussy became wetter and wetter, until, finally, mom said it was time. I moved up over my sister, only partially resting on her, supporting my weight on my arms, and feeling her naked body against mine. Her breasts pushing against my chest, her nipples rock hard. We kissed; Deb responded with real passion, she was on fire.

"Do it, Wayne, I want you in me." She gasped when we finally separated our lips.

"It could hurt, you know, when I take your cherry."

"I don't care about that, it won't hurt for long anyway. I want you in me, I want to have sex, its time. Besides you're not taking my cherry, I'm giving it to you." Deb said before she kissed me again, hard.

"Listen to your sister, Wayne. Debs right, its time. Its time for you to make her a woman. Fuck your sister, she's ready."

Over the last week I'd found you should always listen to your mother. I moved my cock forward, pressing at Debs labia, but they weren't quite open enough to allow me to enter without help opening the way. I was about to reach down when mom intervened. "My babies need help, here Wayne, let me." Mom reached down and, with one hand, opened Debs pussy, exposing her vaginal entrance to me. And, with her other hand, she guided my cock into position. "There, everything's ready, do it, now!"

Finally in position I eased my hips forward, I was so excited. I was entering only my second pussy, and, not only did the pussy belong to a virgin, but it also belonged to my twin sister. Deb was not really any tighter than mom, after all mom hadn't had sex with anything other than her hand since before she'd had us. But the knowledge that no other male had been where I now was, was such a turn on. Then I found the ultimate difference between Deb and mom, my cock reached her hymen. Being used to moms open vagina, even though I was expecting it, my cock being stopped was still a surprise. I didn't know what to do, this was far beyond my experience, I knew I had to break through the barrier, but I didn't want to hurt Deb, at least, I wanted to hurt her as little as possible. So I turned for advice to the one person who'd been through it before. "Mom, I'm there. What do I do now, to make it easier for Deb?"

"That's sweet, you see how considerate your brother is Deb. Wayne, you know how it hurts more when you try to remove a plaster slowly, well this is the same thing, and one quick, sharp pain is better than a lot of smaller pains. Just drive through, let Deb tell you when so she can be ready."

"Okay, Deb. It's up to you, I won't move until you're ready."

"Wayne, I'm ready, believe me I'm more than ready. I've already told you I don't mind the pain. I just want you in me. Do it now!"

Deb gasped when I pulled back and drove at her hymen, it only resisted for a moment and then I was through, balls deep in my sister; she was no longer a virgin. I held myself and asked her how she felt.

"It hurt a bit when you broke through, but not as much as I imagined it would. It still stings a bit. It feels so strange having your pen..., cock, in me like this." Mom laughed, "You think it feels strange having your brother in you like that. How do you think it felt like for me the first time with my son? Well, Wayne, how do you feel now? You've had your cock in both your mother and sister. Not bad for a boy who was a virgin only a week ago."

"I feel like I'm in heaven mom. Now that I've had sex with you both I love you even more, I love you now not only as a son or brother, but also as a man loves his lovers. If I felt like this with another girl I'd want to get married." Before I could continue Deb started to move under me, she was ready, she wanted me to finish what I'd started.

I began to move in my sister again. Slowly, because I knew she would still be tender, but firmly. Nature was taking over, I was now only partially aware of our mother watching us make love. But, somehow it seemed right. After all, if her pussy belonged to me, then my cock belonged to her, if she wanted to share it with another female, even her own daughter it was alright with me. Mom had watched her son taking her daughters virginity, was watching her children make love. That knowledge was almost enough to push me over the edge, I drove harder and faster into Deb.

Debbie was now well lubricated, my cock was now moving smoothly and easily. Her pain had obviously gone, for now at least. All Deb wanted now was for us to finish, for us to come. As I neared my come, not wanting to leave Deb behind, I reached down for her clit. She was so hot, so on edge, so near, that when I found it just one touch was enough. Deb exploded in her first real orgasm, her untried vaginal muscles tightened on my cock, not as hard as moms more practised muscles, but hard enough. She pulled me over the edge with her, I climaxed as well. For the first time Debbies vagina received a males sperm. Spurt after spurt shot into her as I unloaded my cum into my sister for the first time. When we finally finished, we just lay together, exhausted, in a haze of pleasure.

Finally I had to move before my weight became too much for Debbie. I pulled out and slumped to the side, looking down at my soft, wet, cock, I saw that there were only slight traces of blood, of my sisters' virginity. Deb didn't move when I moved off her, except to moan when my cock pulled out of her. She just laid there, her legs still spread wide, her pussy, with some traces of cum and blood around the lips, was already closing as the stimulation left her.

"Wayne," Mom said, attracting my attention. "I think you better go to bed now, I'll look after Debbie. Get a good nights sleep, we'll talk tomorrow."

I bent over and kissed first mom then Debbie, "Goodnight." I said as I got up and left the room.

CHAPTER 6

I was sitting at the table having breakfast the next morning when Debbie came in. "Morning, how are you feeling?" I asked.

Debbie blushed a little before replying, "A little sore, but not too bad."

"I'm glad. You're not sorry about what happened are you?" I asked. Concerned she might, in the light of day, regret what had happened between us. It turned out I didn't have to worry.

"No, Wayne. I'm glad we did it. I've wanted to do it for years, I just hadn't thought about doing it with you. I hope we can do it again. If its okay with mom."

"No problem, Deb," Mom said as she entered the room. "I'm willing to share Wayne. We're just going to have to be careful no one finds out about what we're doing."

"I certainly agree with that Mom," I said as I went and kissed her. "I love you both, even more now, I don't want anything coming between us."

"You're so right. Now, since Debs now involved I think its fair she has the same rules I do. From now on her pussy belongs to you, Deb, do you agree that your brother can do what he wants with your pussy from now on?" Debbie just nodded, mom continued. "Okay, you can only wear your panties during your period, other than then it must be uncovered and available to Wayne whenever he wants it, just like mine."

"Mom," I interrupted, "I think that we'd better make a slight difference with Debbie. While we're still at school she can wear panties during the week, but she must take them off as soon as she gets home."

"Yes, that's a good idea, it would be almost impossible for Deb to conceal the fact she wasn't wearing panties at school. And we don't want to attract any attention. Okay, but that's the only difference, do you agree Debbie?" Again Debbie just nodded, obviously she was still a little overwhelmed with what had and was still happening. But she was obviously willing to accept my control over her most private parts. I just sat back letting mom take control, waiting to see what would come next. "You know Debbie, there's no school today, its Saturday. Take off your panties, you won't need them again until Monday." Debbie was reaching under her skirt to pull her panties down when mom stopped her. "Come on Debbie, hold your skirt up, let your brother see you pulling them off. After all, you're not hiding anything he hasn't seen before. You might as well start getting used to Wayne looking at your body, he's going to see it a lot from now on."

Debbie stood up, she held her skirt with one hand, exposing her panties, and then, she started to pull them down with the other. It was immediately obvious that she needed both hands free to remove her panties easily. As soon as she noticed this mom reached over and held the skirt. With both hands now free Deb was able to remove her panties. I watched as she slowly uncovered her pussy, the sight of my sister taking off her panties, together with our conversation, had an obvious effect on me. The only problem was I wanted to give Deb a little more time to recover from the pain of losing her virginity. Still, I thought, there is mom, and Debbie could help.

By now Deb was standing there naked from the waist down, mom was still holding her skirt up. She blushed a little when she saw me examining her body. "You look beautiful Debbie." I said. "Have you ever thought about shaving your pubic hair?"

"No, do you want me too?" Deb asked. "I will if you want."

"It would be nice, I'll leave the decision up to you. Before you decide lets see what it would look like. Mom, lift up your dress, show Debbie what she would look like shaved."

Mom immediately dropped Debbie's skirt and raised the front of her dress, exposing her lower body to us. "See, Debbie, would you like to look like that?"

"I must admit it looks sexy, with no hair at all."

"It feels sexy too." I said. Before she knew what was happening, I'd taken Debbie's hand and was running it over moms bare mound. "Feel how smooth it is, the only problem is it has to be shaved often, to keep it like this. But that's fun too." Then, moving her hand down further I added, "And feel how different her pussy feels to yours." By now her hand was running over our mothers' pussy. It was obvious that neither mom nor Deb minded, so I pushed on. "Debbie why don't you get mom ready for me."

"What do you mean," she asked. "I don't know what you want me to do."

"Masturbate her, do it like you would do to yourself. Play with her pussy until she's wet enough for me to enter her." I took my hand away from hers, leaving it resting on moms pussy, and waited.

It didn't take long before Debbie was moving her hand in caressing strokes on moms' pussy. She kept her eyes on our mothers face the whole time, what she saw must of reassured her because she relaxed and concentrated on moms pussy. She ran her fingers up and down our mothers slit, before parting the labia with her other hand, exposing moms vaginal entrance and clit. When Debs finger circled moms' entrance and dipped slightly inside, I leaned forward, and whispered in her ear. "Isn't it amazing we both came out of that little hole you have your finger in." Debbie redoubled her efforts, efforts which from the moisture now coating her fingers were being very successful. When she started to move towards the clit I knew I had to stop her. "That's enough Deb, she's ready." I moved Debbie's hand out of our mothers' crotch, mom moaned when I did so; she'd been so ready, so nearly there. But now it was my turn.

I leaned mom over the table, flipping her dress up over her back. Mom spread her legs to improve my access. I dropped my pants and moved into position, ready to take my mother again. "Debbie," I said, "Open moms pussy for me, and guide me in."

Immediately Debbie dropped to her knees beside us. With one hand she spread moms' labia the other grasped my cock. Then, carefully, she guided me home. Once I felt the head of my cock penetrate mom I drove in, hard. Mom grunted as she was pushed against the table, but she pushed back, welcoming my cock into her body. Once more mom and I began to make love. Debbie was still on her knees beside us, so I knew she was getting a good view. She was only inches away from our joined organs; Deb was watching her brothers' cock moving in and out of her mothers' pussy, watching moms labia move in and out with my cock. I realised after a few minutes that I was going to come soon. I reached down for moms clit, but Debbie stopped me, "I'll do it, you just concentrate on finishing." As Debbie reached for moms clit I grasped her hips and intensified my thrusting, driving myself to climax. Debbie was obviously doing a good job as mom started gasping, "Yes! Oh yes!" she was going over the edge. I joined her. I drove as deep as I could into my mother and locked her in place with my hands as I, as we came. I pumped my load into her as she came screaming.

As I lay there, slumped over moms back, my softening cock still buried inside her, I felt my cum and moms juice beginning to run down our thighs. Then, suddenly, I felt Debbie's tongue; she was licking up the results of our mating. I could feel her collecting all the juice from my thighs, then, after a slight hesitation, she began cleaning my balls. It was a real turn on. Here I was, my cock buried in my mothers' pussy, and my sister was licking my balls. I reached down and pulled her head away. "What are you doing, I was having fun." She complained. I just told her she'd been doing a good job, but moms' pussy needed a little cleaning too. I guided her head back between our legs. She didn't hesitate; her tongue resumed its attack on my balls. But this time Deb started lapping towards mom, then she was no longer lapping at me, she was licking moms' pussy! I wanted to see this! I slowly pulled out of mom, when I was clear Debbie had full access to our mother, she took advantage of it. It was an incredible sight, my sister eating her own mothers' pussy. I moved over and kissed mum, asking her if Deb was doing a good job. "God, yes! She's even better at it than you are." I didn't mind that, after all she had a pussy of her own; she had more experience pleasuring one than I did, even if it was her own. By now mom was starting to moan, "Yes, yes, yes. That's it Debbie, that's it. I'm almost there, now, now, do it now!" I looked down and saw Deb move her attack to moms' clitoris. Her tongue flicking rapidly at the swollen knob, finally she took it between her lips and sucked, hard. Mom came just as hard. As mom was coming down from her climax Debbie gave her pussy a few more licks, more I think to collect some more juice, and ease her pussy down from its high, and stood up, licking her lips, her face was covered with mom and mine combined juices, she'd never looked prettier, or sexier. "I want you, now!" she said taking my cock in her hand.

I reached down and removed her hand. "I want you, too. But it's too soon. You're still too tender, I don't want to hurt you again. Wait until tomorrow, take a couple of hot baths, they should help."

"But Wayne, I need it now, I'm so hot." She whined.

"I didn't say I won't help relieve you, I just won't penetrate you, yet. Here sit on the table."

Debbie sat down immediately. She automatically pulled up her skirt and spread her legs, exposing herself to us without a blush. As I looked between her legs I could tell she was more than ready. Her labia were engorged with blood, spreading apart revealing her vaginal entrance. She was reacting as nature intended, she was a female ready to mate. I looked over at mom and saw that she was staring also. It was obvious what she wanted to do. And I wanted it too. "Go on, mom, she's waiting for you. Help your little girl. Debbie needs to come."

Hearing my words, Deb, looked at mom, "Please mom, I want you too. I need you too!"

That was all mom needed, she moved forward, sinking to her knees, inches from her daughters pussy. Debbie lifted her legs, put them over moms' shoulders, and pulled moms face into her crotch. Mom instantly extended her tongue and began eating her daughters' pussy. She dove in with a vengeance, her tongue gathering up Debs abundant juices, she was so wet mom actually had to swallow before she could continue. I watched for a while entranced with the sight of a mother and daughter making love. And that's what was happening, as with me, mom was expressing her love to her child, both as a mother, and a lover.

I was rock hard again, I couldn't enter mom in her position so I decided to introduce Debbie to the other type of oral sex, between a man and a woman. I moved up alongside her head, and began rubbing my cock over her face. Debbie immediately got the idea; she took my cock in her hand and guided it into her mouth. She closed her lips over the shaft and started to suck. I told her to use her tongue, and she started sweeping it around the head of my cock. After a while she tried to move her head back and forward on my cock, unfortunately because of the position she was in, there was very little movement she could make. Realising she wanted me to come, I started to move my cock in and out of her mouth. Fucking her mouth as I had her pussy the night before. When I finally told her I was about to come, I asked her if she wanted me to pull out. Debbie reached up when I was on an outstroke and grabbed my butt, holding me still. She immediately attacked the head of my cock with quick, sharp, strokes, obviously wanting me to come in her mouth. It worked. Spurt after spurt of my cum shot out of my cock into her waiting mouth. Deb swallowed again, and again, as my load filled her mouth. Then she stiffened as her own climax swept through her body. Debbie relaxed her grip and my cock flopped out of her mouth. She laid there, a smile of satisfaction on her face.

Mom stood, her face glazed with her daughters juices. "That was delicious, if I'd known eating a woman would be so nice I'd have tried it before." Then she kissed me. "Thanks for letting this happen. I don't suppose you have anything left for me?" Mom asked, as she caressed my cock and balls.

"I'm afraid not, at least for a while. Debbie got everything I had."

"Oh well, I guess I can wait awhile. I mean there's no rush."

Debbie quickly sat up, she pulled mom to her, opening her mouth she showed us a small white pool resting on her tongue, she hadn't swallowed her last mouthful of cum. Mom smiled, "You are such a considerate daughter, saving mother a nice snack. It looks delicious." Moms' mouth closed over Debbies in a very French kiss. Her tongue plundering Debs mouth. When they finally pulled apart, before Deb closed her mouth, I could see there was no longer any trace of my sperm, mom had gotten it all.

"Well, Wayne. That was a nice way to spend a morning. What do you have planned for your sister and me for the rest of the day?"

"Actually, nothing. Before we do anything else I want Debbie to heal a bit so there will be no pain. But tomorrow, ah tomorrow I have some plans for then."

CHAPTER 7

The next morning I woke mom and Debbie bright and early, we had a lot to do before we went to church. First we had a nice hot shower, your morning shower is a totally different experience when you're sharing it with 2 women. I really enjoyed the washing I gave and received. Just thinking about washing my sister and mother was a turn on; I was hard before we got in the shower. But that would have to wait.

The previous evening Debbie had decided that she wanted to be shaved. So, once we were dried off mom and I took Deb into her bedroom and shaved her as she lay naked on her bed. Then, when I was finished, I told them that I wanted to be shaved as well. I took Debs place and they shaved me, at least they didn't have to hold my cock out of the way, it was fully erect the whole time. Once I was done we touched up mom, shaving away her stubble.

When we were finished, we went to moms' room and stood in front of her full-length mirror. What a sight. A naked son, standing between his equally naked mother and sister, looking at themselves in the mirror. All three shaved bare. I ran my eyes up and down my lovers bodies, knowing they were doing the same thing. Taking in their breasts, hardened nipples pointing back at me. Moving down to their bare, tight-lipped pussies. The pussies I had full access too. "God, you two look beautiful." I said as I reached down and ran a finger up and down each of their now bald slits. They automatically reached for my cock, "You're not so bad yourself." Mom replied. Debbie just smiled.

"From now on I want us to stay shaved. It's a symbol of our connection to each other. We can shave each other every other morning, just like today." I said. They both agreed at once. Before we could do anything else I realised we'd be late for church if we didn't hurry, so we rushed to our rooms to get ready. We had a quick breakfast and then it was time to go.

Before we left the house I stopped them and simply said, "Panty check." Mom realised first what I meant, and, smiling, she raised the front of her dress. I reached out and lightly stroked her bare pussy. Then I turned to Debbie; she had her skirt raised ready for my inspection. Sure enough she had followed the rules. I stroked her pussy as well and led my family out to the car. Nothing more happened until we got home.

As soon as we got in the door mom said, "Thank God." She unbuttoned her dress and let it fall to the floor, stepping out of it. Revealing she was totally naked, she hadn't even worn her bra. "That feels so much better, I felt so wicked, sitting there in church, naked under my dress. Just wanting to go home and have sex with my children." Debbie, not to be out done, was also stripping off her clothes. She had been wearing her bra, but she quickly removed it, adding it to the pile of clothes on the floor. "You're so right mom, I don't think anything could be sexier than sitting in church, listening to the sermon, surrounded by people, without my panties on." Mom just laughed. "There is one thing. Last week, before we went to church, Wayne and I made love in the shower. All the time I was in church I could feel his cum trickling out of my pussy. What a turn on." Turning to me, mom asked, "Don't you think you're a little over dressed?" I agreed. My clothes quickly joined the pile on the floor.

"You know mom, since everyone is comfortable like this, why not make this the way we don't dress when we're at home alone, no one can see through the windows. If anyone comes we could quickly throw on some clothes. Besides, we've been here 4 months already and we've had no visitors anyway, so why shouldn't we be comfortable when we're home. After all we've nothing to hide from each other anymore."

"Ok, Wayne. It's a deal. From now on this is a no clothes zone. Except for panties during periods. Ok, Debbie?" Deb nodded. "Right, now that's settled what do you have planned for today, Wayne?"

"Well, first, since we're already dressed for it, I thought we might sunbathe for a while, we need to get rid of these white patches. At least some of us do." I added looking at moms tanned body, at least except for the pale patch where her pubic hair had been. She just laughed and said, "Lead the way."

Once we were outside, I got mom to lie down on her towel so Deb and I could put her suntan oil on. We started with her back. You know, I think that one of the most sensuous acts you can do is to oil up your lovers body, be it with massage oil or suntan oil. Running your hands over his or her naked body, caressing it as you rub the oil into the skin. Mom moaned softly as Deb and I covered her from head to toe, then, when we finished, she eagerly turned over. If it had been hot applying the lotion to her back, this was 10 times more exciting, for all of us. Really, the oil was just an excuse to run our hands over her body, and she knew it. She had to. After as Deb was rubbing her oil in areas I'd already worked on, and vice versa, especially her breasts and pussy. I loved rubbing the oil onto her pussy, Deb obviously did too. Finally, all good things must come to an end. Mom rose, her body glistening in the sun, and Debbie took her place. As we rubbed the first oil on Debbies' back, I looked over at mom, she smiled, leaned over, and we kissed. Mom was as eager to oil Debbies' pussy as De had been with her. After we finished Debbie I eagerly took her place. If it had been good rubbing the oil onto someone you loved, imagine what it was like being the recipient of the attention. There I was lying down, my eyes closed as four hands gently applied oil to my back, rubbing in slow, smooth, soft, motions. Caressing me, loving me. And it was the two women I loved most in the world who were doing it, my mother and sister. Then it was time to turn over. I lay back watching them work. They looked like two gilded statues in the sunlight, but there hands weren't cold like metal, far from it. They were totally into what they were doing to me. In a way we were learning about each others body, since we were so totally open to each other. They saved my cock for last, then both moved onto it at the same time. I'm telling you it's a feeling that has to be felt to be believed. Four hands rubbing, caressing, suntan oil onto my genitals, working away at my cock and balls, until, when they finished, I was as shiny as they were. They looked at me hungrily, waiting for me to make the next move. But it wasn't time. So I just said "Let's not waste the oil, 20 minutes each side then in the pool." I set the timer we used to make sure we didn't burn, and lay down to catch some rays. Realising I wasn't going to make a move, they took up a place on either side of me and did the same. It was hard not making a move on them, but if things worked out like I hoped, it would be worth it.

After we finished sunbathing, we dove in the pool to cool off, though the water wouldn't really cool down the real heat we were suffering from. We swam and played for about half an hour, though it's a little hard to swim with a hard on as I found out. Whenever we were close enough to each other little touches were exchanged, initially just on an arm or a leg, later they grew more intimate. I found myself running my hand over a breast, or cupping it for an instant before giving it a squeeze and letting go. I knew mom and Debbie were doing the same. When our touches moved to the genital area I knew it was time. I called mom and Deb over to the side of the pool, we stood there for a minute, our hands occupied under water, my hands cupping their pussies, theirs holding my cock. I kissed them and said, "Lets dry off."

We climbed out of the pool, grabbed our towels and quickly dried off. Once we were finished I just said one word, "Bedroom." That was all it took. It was a race to get inside and upstairs. We must have been a sight, (luckily there was no one to see it!) a naked mother running into the house pursued by her equally naked daughter and son. The sons erect penis bouncing as he chased after his females, it was just like a wildlife program. An elaborate mating ritual. When I entered the bedroom mom and Debbie were standing at the foot of the bed, waiting. They didn't have long to wait.

I placed a pillow at the bottom of the bed, and another at about head height. "Okay, mom, lie down on the bed with your butt on the edge."

Mom immediately assumed the position, spreading her legs; the pillow raised her pussy, presenting it for penetration, but not yet! "Deb, lie down on top of mom, put your legs outside of hers." Without any hesitation Debbie followed my instructions, seeing that she wasn't very stable I told mom to hold on to her. She did, but not in the way I'd anticipated. Mom didn't hold Debbie around the waist, instead she held her with a hand on each breast. I stood back and looked at the treat I'd constructed. My sister, on top of our mother, her breasts held in moms' hands. Their legs spread, one on top of the other. Their pussies only inches apart, they even looked alike, their tight labia slightly spread by the position of their legs, a trace of lubrication forming. Two women almost ready to have sex. It was now my job to finish getting them ready and then give them what they wanted, indeed needed. And in the position I'd placed them I could move from one to the other very easily.

I went to my knees between their legs, ready to prepare them for penetration, not that it appeared they needed much preparation. I started by stimulating moms' labia with my tongue, while at the same time doing the same to Debbies' with my fingers. The first contact brought moans from them, they were both so wet, I realised I could enter them now. But I wanted to play a little first, to tease them. I moved my mouth from pussy to pussy, always keeping the other on edge with my fingers. Finally I decided it was time for me to move to the next stage. Standing, I bent over and kissed them both, asking if they wanted something else. "God, yes." mom replied. "Fuck me, I want you now!"

Since I was a good boy I always did what my mother said, yeah right! I took Debbies' hand, put it on her pussy, and told her to hold the lips open ready for me, when it was her turn. Then, I ran my cock up and down moms slit to lubricate the head with her juices. Finally I was ready. I moved my cock into position, pushed forward, through her engorged labia, and I slid deep into moms' vagina, mom released a loud sigh of contentment as she felt me enter her. I slowly thrust in her once, twice, three times, then holding open her pussy lips I pulled out, leaving her gaping pussy I moved up, lined up with Debbies' open hole and drove in. This time it was Debbies' turn to sigh. Again I gave her three thrusts before withdrawing and moving back to mom. I established an easy rhythm, moving from one to the other, always stimulating the clit of the one I was not penetrating. As I continued I realised that just over a week ago I was a virgin, wondering if and when I'd get laid. Now, that was no longer a problem, now I was getting all the sex an 18 year old could want. Here I was making love to two women at the same time, and not just any women, my mother and sister. I loved them so much, so much more than I had before. And they loved me enough to share their bodies with me. It was too much for me. I had to come. I drove harder into mom, and attacked her clit. She was right on the edge too and that pushed her over. Her vaginal muscles contracted on my cock as she came, that did it for me, I felt the familiar feeling of my cum welling up from my balls. The first spurt of cum shot into moms' depths, not wanting to leave Debbie out I immediately started to pull out of mom. "No, Wayne! Don't." she moaned as she felt me begin to withdraw from her. Her muscles clamped down, trying to hold me inside her, but I managed to escape, shooting another spurt into her as I did so. Quickly, holding onto my cock tightly, I entered Debbie, as I released my cock the remainder of my load shot into her. Then it was her turn to come. She was tighter than mom, but conversely her vaginal muscles weren't as strong. It was still a snug fit.

Realising it was now time for the next stage of my plan, I pulled Debbie to her feet, my cock still deep inside her, and then, over her protests I withdrew from her pussy. I covered her pussy with my hand to keep my cum from spilling out and guided her onto the bed, where I moved her back on top of mom, this time positioning her head over moms pussy so that they were in the traditional 69 position. Then I stepped back and waited. I didn't have long to wait; they both started eating the pussy I'd placed in front of them. There before me was most mens dream, two women making love to each other, eating each others pussy, eating my cum out of each other. And, to make it better, they were my own mother and sister. I loved them both, and seeing them make love to each other, while hearing their soft moans really turned me on. I watched them for about ten minutes, I wanted to mount them again, but I wasn't able too, it was too soon, so I decided to interrupt them and let Debbie do the job for me.

They moaned when I pulled Debbie off of mom. I turned her around so that they were lying breast to breast, then I slightly adjusted Debs hips so her pussy would rub against moms. To make sure everything was right I slipped my hand between them, between their pussies. There I was my hand sandwiched between two pussies, it was an unreal feeling, but that wasn't why I had them like this. I removed my hand and whispered in Debbies' ear, "Fuck her, Deb. Fuck mom." Realising what I wanted, Debbie began to grind her pussy against moms, mom, immediately hooked her legs around Debs like she would with me, and started to move against her. They kissed, deep and hard as they moved toward orgasm. From my position I could see the lips of their pussies mash against each other, their juices running down their thighs. Then the tone of their cries changed, they were coming. It was beautiful, watching mother and daughter come together, each having brought the other off. After a while, mom whispered something to Debbie, and then they stood up and took my hands.

"Come here, Wayne. Deb and I want to thank you." She guided me to the bed and I lay down. Mom and Debbie took position on either side of me; mom reached down and took hold of my cock. "Lets see what we can do with this, Debbie."

That was the last thing she said for some time. She guided my cock into her mouth and started sucking it to hardness. While she was doing that, Debbie, bent down and started licking my balls. All this attention certainly had the desired effect. I quickly became as hard as I'd ever been. That's when mom let me out of her mouth, she leaned down and began running her tongue up and down my shaft. When Debbie saw what mom was doing, she abandoned my balls and started doing the same to the other side of my cock. Their tongues danced up and down, when they reached the top, their lips met in a kiss that engulfed the head of my cock, exposing it to the stimulation of both of their tongues. Then they would resume their titillation of the shaft. Before long I felt the approach of my climax, I think I told them I was coming, I'm not sure, I was so turned on, so ready to come. And come I did, the first spurt shot out, landing on my stomach, mom and Debbie made no attempt to capture my load, they just kept licking as spurt after spurt followed, covering my lower stomach with globs of cum.

Finally I finished shooting, they met for a final kiss, and cleaned off the head of my cock. Then, they separated, and started lapping up the cum from my stomach. I couldn't believe what I was seeing, my mother and sister, licking up my cum, like a cat with a saucer of milk.

When they finished they moved up next to me, we kissed, I could taste the mixture of their juices and my cum. We were done for now, and I knew there wouldn't be anything more happening today, I put my arms around them and we curled up against each other and went to sleep.

CHAPTER 8

The next week mom got us a new, bigger, bed. We've all slept together since then. This week in a way was our honeymoon. It was one thrill after another, we tried everything we could think of, and we could think of a lot, we made love whenever we could. I tried to make sure that mom and Debbie had all of the cum they wanted, whenever I could get an erection I'd mount one of them. We didn't mind where we were, we just wanted to get my cum into their pussies, and bring them off. It seemed to me that they both wanted my cum in there bodies the whole time, I tried to oblige, I was one happy teenage boy that week. Mostly it was just variations of what we'd tried before, but there were some wonderful exceptions.

Monday morning, as we were going to school, I stopped Debbie at the door. I wanted to make her day more exciting. I pulled her into my arms and we kissed, I dropped my hand under her skirt and caressed her pussy. Then I moved her to the wall, still kissing her, and pulled her panty crotch to the side, just enough to bare her pussy and allow me to enter her. I opened my zipper, and pulled out my cock, I was already fully erect. Positioning myself, I told Debbie to guide me in. She did immediately, as she fitted me into her hole I drove forward, pushing her up against the wall, her butt bouncing back and forth with my strokes, until, finally, I came. I thrust deeply into her and held her tightly to me as I shot my cum deep into her vagina. When I finally finished coming I pulled out and straightened her panties. "There, that should give you a fun time at school."

We don't have any classes together but I usually see Deb quite often in the hall as our lockers are close to each others. Today whenever I saw her she was usually either going into or coming out of the bathroom. Later, after we got home, I got the full details about what had happened.

"All morning I could feel your cum trickling out of my pussy, making the crotch of my panties wet. During homeroom I had to ask to go to the bathroom. When I got there I took off my panties and put the crotch in my mouth so I could suck up your cum. Just knowing I was eating your cum in the school bathroom made me play with my pussy, I had to come. I heard a couple of other girls come in, I couldn't stop. Luckily the panties stopped me making any noise when I came. I then quickly put my panties back on and went back to class. I had to do it 4 or 5 times this morning. I got so hot, sitting in class, surrounded with my classmates, with my brothers sperm in my pussy, I was sure I could smell your cum, and my arousal. I was sure everyone else could too, and that they knew I'd just had sex. I even touched myself through my skirt a few times when no one could see what I was doing. Please don't do it again Wayne. I could hardly concentrate on my work. I don't want to fail any tests. I would have, if there'd been one today." I just laughed and told her not to worry, it was only a oncer; I wouldn't touch her again before school.

We went out to dinner one night and I decided to take advantage of the tinted windows. On the way there mom drove, I was in the back seat with Debbie. It was a bit cramped, but I was able to mount her successfully and bring us to climax just before we got to the restaurant. The movement of the car, and just knowing where we were made it even more exciting. We had a corner table against the wall, so I had Debbie sit at the back where no one could see what she was doing. We had spaghetti so she could eat one handed. Her other hand was under her pussy, collecting the cum that was flowing out of her. After desert mom got to lick her hand clean. The seat where she'd been sitting was still a little damp but we didn't care. On the way back Debbie drove, it was moms turn in the back seat with me. After we parked the car, Debbie got her snack of cum when she cleaned up moms' pussy.

Two days later I had a free period after lunch so I went to have lunch with mom. I got her to give her secretary an extra hour for lunch so we could have some time together after we got back. We had a couple of hotdogs and went back to her building. There were a lot of people waiting at one of the lifts so we went to the other one, and, naturally that one came first. Mom and I moved to the back of the lift, and everyone else crowded in behind us, I stood behind her. I quickly looked around and saw that no one would see me doing anything, so I decided to enjoy the ride.

I nudged one of moms' feet; she moved it slightly to the side. Then I carefully raised the back of her dress enough for my hand to slip under. I reached between her legs for her pussy. I cupped it in my hand, caressing it with a circular motion all the way up to her floor. It was a long, slow ride, but we both enjoyed it thoroughly, at least I know I did, and judging by her juices covering my hand, so did she. Finally, all good things must come to an end, we arrived at our destination. I quickly pulled my hand out and we exited the lift.

When we got into her office mom quickly kissed me. "That was so naughty of you, Wayne. Playing with me like that. All I could think of was that here I was surrounded with people and my son was playing with my pussy. It was such a turn on."

"That's good, mom. I've still got another hour, lets see what we can do now."

I led her to her chair and sat her in it. Then I knelt before her and raised her dress exposing her pussy, she was really aroused, the lips were engorged and parting, her thighs were shimmering with a sheen of pussy juice. It was a delicious sight. I wanted dessert. I commenced running my tongue in broad sweeps up and down her slit, I was just getting into it when there was a knock at the door. I quickly looked around, and, seeing that the desk had a solid front I moved into the desk cavity, mom pulled her chair into position. "Come," she said.

"Mrs. Williamson, I have the proposal you wanted." I heard a voice say. As they started to talk I decided to have some fun.

I pushed moms dress up and moved her legs apart, resuming my attack on her pussy, this time knowing she didn't dare make a sound. I dove into her depths, eating her for all I was worth. Moms' conversation became strained, until finally she told whoever was talking to her that she would read the proposal and get back to them.

As soon as the door closed she grabbed my head and pulled it out of her crotch. "God, Wayne, you got me so hot, I need you in me. Now!"

I quickly went and locked the door while mom pulled her blinds. Then I cleared off her desk and helped her lie on it. I paused, taking in the sight before me, mom, lying on her desk, legs spread waiting for me to mount her, I didn't make her wait long. I guided my cock to her entrance and slowly penetrated her. It was so hot, knowing that while we were making love there were people working only feet away. We were both so hot that we didn't last long, mom had to bite her lip to keep from screaming as we both came, my cum filling her vagina. After we had recovered, I kissed mom and told her I'd see her tonight. Then I left saying goodbye to her secretary who was just getting back to her desk. Leaving mom to spend the rest of the afternoon with my cum in her belly.

Then, just before the weekend I came home and found Debbie wearing her panties, her period had arrived. When mom arrived I discovered she had begun hers as well. I wasn't surprised that they had them at the same time. I'd read somewhere that women who live together often have their periods at the same time. I guess its probably natures way of making sure that they would be fertile at the same time, so their cycles would be in sync. Mom later told me she'd taken her panties to work because she was expecting her period. Both mom and Debbie have always been as regular as clockwork.

I don't know if they expected our sexual action to stop, but I didn't care about a little blood, and they were more than willing to keep going. The only thing we didn't do was oral sex, at least at first. That changed when I came home one day and found them eating each other out. When they finished there were some traces of blood on their faces and I joked that I was in love with two vampires. They just laughed and said it wasn't so bad, and I should try it sometime. I did, they were right.

It was just before their periods ended that they dropped a bombshell. Mom and Debbie were sitting at the table and they asked me to sit down. When I did, mom continued. "Wayne, Debbie and I would like you to do something for us." She said.

"Of course mom, I'll do anything you want. You know that." I told her.

"I sure hope so. Wayne, Debbie and I both want to have your baby."

CHAPTER 9

I couldn't believe what I'd just heard. "What did you say?" I gasped.

"Debbie and I want you to make us both pregnant. I discovered I was sorry when I got my period, that's when I realised I wanted another baby, I wanted your baby. I talked to Debbie about it, asking her if she'd mind me having your baby. Deb thought about it for a while, then told me she'd have no problem with it, so long as she could have your baby too."

"That's right, Wayne. I love you, I want to have your baby." Debbie confirmed.

"But," mom continued, "if you don't want to, it's alright. Debbie and I will just go on birth control and we can continue just like before. It's up to you."

I sat there thinking it through, with mom and Debbie waiting for my answer. Make my mother and sister pregnant, deliberately. It was a wild idea. Though, I must admit, it was really only taking our actions to the next logical stage. Still the thought…. Then I realised that the thought was turning me on, my body was reacting, it had already made up its mind and was waiting for my brain to catch up. There was still one problem I could think of. "Mom, what about Debbie and college. I don't want her to miss going to college."

"Mom and I have talked about it. If I get pregnant I'll only have to miss a few days around my delivery. Mom will hire a nanny to look after the babies during weekdays when we're at work and school. We can look after them overnight and during the weekends."

"Are you both sure? I mean this is much more serious than just making love, this is creating new life? Mom, do you really want to have your sons' baby? Debbie, do you really want to have your brothers baby?"

They both simultaneously responded, "Yes." They had obviously made up their minds. And so, I realised had I. "Okay, I'll try to get you pregnant." Suddenly my arms were full as they hugged and kissed me. "Thank you, Wayne. You don't know how much this means to us." Mom said, tears streaming down her cheeks.

We immediately got down to the mechanics of how we'd do it. It was decided that until they began to become fertile again, we'd abstain from sex so I wouldn't waste any sperm. They wanted it all in their pussies when it might do its job. Then, when it was time, I'd have sex with one of them in the morning and one in the evening. Giving myself a chance to rebuild a load before the next one.

The next few days were very hard, and so was I. Looking at their naked bodies all the time, and not being able to touch them, and knowing why was driving me mad. I couldn't wait for my chance to do my duty.

Finally the day arrived. Mom and Debbie asked me to leave the bedroom so they could get ready. After about 25 minutes or so, Debbie came to get me, "Moms ready for you."

She told me.

When I entered the bedroom I entered a wonderland. They had pulled the curtains and filled the room with fragrant candles. The candles bathed the bed with their flickering light, and, lying in the middle of the bed, her hips raised on a pillow so my load would get as deep into her as possible, her legs spread wide, was my mother. Waiting for her son to make her pregnant. The lips of her pussy were engorged and parted, I realised what Deb had meant about mom being ready. Obviously Deb had gone down on her. Debbie came up behind me; I felt her breasts pressing into my back as she put her arms around me. "We wanted this 1st time to be special." She said.

"It's always special with either of you." I replied.

"I know. But this time it's not just for fun like before. This time we're trying to have a baby."

Debbie was right. Before, I'd assumed that they were on birth control, so I didn't worry about pregnancy. Now, for the first time, not only did I know they weren't on birth control, but we were actually trying to create a new life.

Debbie reached down and grabbed my cock. "Come on, Wayne. Lets get the show on the road." She led me to the bed. "I'll guide you in when you're ready."

I climbed onto the bed and positioning between moms legs, lowered myself onto her waiting body, her breasts squashed against my chest as I kissed her. "Are you sure mom?" I asked. Mom smiled at me and nodded. It was time. "Okay, Debbie."

I felt Debbie grasp my cock again; she guided it to moms open pussy, and then ran the head up and down moms slit to lubricate it. Once she was satisfied she directed it to the opening of our mothers vagina. She lodged the head inside the entrance and released my cock. Bending down she said, "There you go Wayne. It's all yours. Give me another brother or sister." Kissing mom and my cheeks she moved back off the bed.

I thrust into moms' depths; she was so warm and wet, so ready, so eager, so hot. I commenced a slow steady pattern, mom arched up to receive each thrust, trying to get me deeper and deeper into her body. It was as if she was trying to get me back into her womb. She gasped into my ear, "Do it, Wayne! Do it! Give me your baby!"

If she was trying to fire me up it wasn't needed. Just knowing that I might be about to make my own mother pregnant was all I needed to be hotter than ever before. I realised then that I wanted to her to have my baby. I wanted to watch her belly grow with my child. I wanted to plant a child in the same womb I'd been created in. And I realised I wouldn't be much longer. I could feel my sperm begin to rise from my balls, this time to begin the race to create new life. I gasped that I was coming and I drove deep one final time; mom locked her legs around me holding me in place. I came, harder than ever before, shooting my sperm as deep into my mothers belly as I possibly could. Trying to penetrate her womb with it, trying to impregnate her. Spurt after spurt erupted from my cock, until I was finally spent. When she realised I was no longer ejaculating into her mom relaxed her legs, this was a signal she had obviously worked out with Debbie. Deb quickly pulled me off mom and placed another pillow under her hips, raising them even higher, trying to help my sperm get even deeper. Mom was laying there, her legs still spread, her pussy slowly closing. Smiling at me mom said, "Thank you, Wayne. I'll just lie here for the next half hour or so to give your sperm their chance. You better go and get breakfast ready."

Debbie and I went downstairs, "That was beautiful, Wayne. Just imagine, I might have seen you and mom create a new brother or sister for me. I can't wait for tonight."

Sure enough, half an hour later mom joined us for breakfast. Looking at her as she came in, it was amazing to think that inside her body my sperm was racing to find her egg and create a new life. If it already hadn't. I asked her what she'd do when my cum started trickling out.

"It won't." she replied. "When I got up I put my diaphragm in, to make sure your sperm stayed there all day."

Debbie laughed, "That's wild mom, using a birth control device to help you get pregnant. I'll have to get one too, so I can do the same."

"Already taken care of baby. I bought two, I'll give you yours tonight, after.."

We finished breakfast and headed off, I was already looking forward to trying to impregnate Debbie. All through school I was thinking about what had happened that morning, I had actually tried to get my mother pregnant! Mom might even now be carrying my child. And my sister might be next.

That night was a repeat of my time with mom. The only difference being that I was in the room from the beginning. I was there while mom was getting Debbie ready for me. It was an erotic experience, watching my mother (who was possibly already carrying my child) preparing my sister for her first chance at becoming pregnant.

This time mom led me to bed telling me to make her a grandmother. And, when I gave Debbie her chance to stop and she refused, I sure tried. Because it was evening Debbie stayed with her hips elevated for over an hour. She inserted her diaphragm before we went to sleep. As I lay there between my mother and sister the last thing I thought of before I dropped off was that I might now be sleeping with two pregnant women, two women carrying my children.

With the exception of the candles we continued with this pattern for the remainder of their fertile period, though they sometimes swapped between morning and evening. On their most fertile days we all stayed home and made love time and time again, whenever I could get an erection, hoping we'd succeed.

Finally the day for the start of their periods arrived, we waited through the day; it was a Saturday, which was fortunate because the tension would have made it impossible to concentrate at work or school. Finally, that evening, we began to hope. Neither of them had ever been this late in starting, in fact mom had only ever not had her period once by now. Guess when that was. Mom and Debbie went upstairs with their pregnancy tests. It was the longest few minutes of my life.

There was no expression on their faces when they came back into the room. Then Debbie smiled, "Congratulations, Wayne. You're going to be a father." I was ecstatic; I turned to mom, she just grinned and said, "Snap." Then they were both in my arms, we just stood there hugging, tears of joy running down our faces, we had succeeded, we were going to be parents. As I stood there holding my pregnant lovers I thought that the next nine months are going to be very interesting.

CHAPTER 10

I hadn't thought our lives together could get any better; I was in love and making love with my mother and sister. And they were now both pregnant with my children. I just didn't realise how them being pregnant would add to our sex lives.

The next day I went out and bought several books on pregnancy, I wanted to be ready for what was ahead of us. Mom and Debbie laughed when they saw what I was reading, but I didn't mind, I needed to know what was going to happen. I found out something interesting while reading. I liked the way the pregnant women looked, more than liked. And this was with pictures, which were mainly clothed, or in underwear, I wanted to see some naked. I needed to see some naked.

Later that evening I went on line and started searching. I typed in 'pregnant photos' and started going through the results. Most of the sites were pay sites, but they did have free samples. I was hooked. As soon as I saw the first nude photo I started getting hard. Now, having lived with two naked women for over a month I was used to the naked female form, in other words it was still nice to look at but I no longer became hard every time. I guess it was natures way to protect me. After all otherwise I'd have been hard all the time. But this, this was different. Seeing the bulging bellies was really turning me on. I thought they looked beautiful, probably even more beautiful than if they hadn't been pregnant.

I found myself reaching for my cock; I gently ran my hand up and down the shaft as I moved from picture to picture. Even as I was doing it I realised this was the first time I'd masturbated since we'd started our new relationship. But I didn't care, I needed to come, and soon.

"What are you doing, Wayne?"

I was startled, I hadn't heard mom enter the room. I didn't bother trying to hide what I'd been doing; it was impossible to do that, so I just told her the truth. "I got turned on by these pictures and had to relieve myself."

"Even with your sister and me available, what's so hot?" mom said as she moved over to the computer. "Oh I see. My little boy likes pregnant women. I'm actually glad you do. I was afraid that after Deb and I got bigger you wouldn't want to have sex with us. I know it happens, and I was horny as hell when I was carrying you and your sister. But I can see that won't be a problem, will it? Those are the first pregnant women I've seen naked, except for myself that is, and I must admit I think they're sexy too. Just wait until your sister and I start looking like that."

Suddenly the image flashed into my mind, my mother and sister, their bellies bulging with my children. It was too much I started to come. Mom seeing what was happening quickly dropped to her knees and took my cock into her mouth swallowing my load as soon as it entered her mouth.

Getting to her feet she just said, "You can look at all the pregnant porn you want Wayne, just make sure either your sister or I is here to take care of you." Then she turned and left the room. I just book marked the site and turned off the computer.

Now we didn't only make love, we watched porn together, or more correctly preggy porn, we didn't bother with any other kind. I no longer searched the net for pregnant photos, instead every Friday we would all relax and wind down from the week watching adult movies, adult pregnant movies. We had plenty of movies to watch. Mom had gone out and purchased every pregnant sex movie she could find, then she ordered them on line, we had quite a collection. I wasn't the only one being turned on by the videos either. Both Debbie and mom were just as stimulated as I was, of course I knew they loved each other, and loved making love to each other, but I hadn't thought they would be turned on by pregnant women too. But they obviously were, our sessions after the videos were always the hottest of the week, we all looked forward to them. Then mom said she'd found a special video, we couldn't wait to see it.

It started out like usual, a beautiful, pregnant woman having sex, and then it happened. She started to breast feed her lover, she held his head to her breast and he started suckling at her nipple. It was obvious she was producing milk, you could see some, trickling down her breast. I'd never thought of drinking breast milk, but as I sat there I found myself licking my lips, wishing I was the one taking her breast. I was determined that I would be. "Mom, when you can, could I drink your milk?"

"Of course you can, you both can, why do you think I showed you this. I fed you as babies, and, almost every time, I had an orgasm."

"You can drink mine too," Debbie added, "I'd love to have my brother and mother drinking my milk. How long do we have to wait until we can?"

"I don't know," Mom replied, "my milk came in not too long before you were born. But I read a pamphlet that said milk production could be started by stimulation of the nipple."

With breast milk now our goal we made our plans, we'd wait until after the first trimester, to give their bodies a chance to adjust to the changes they were undergoing, then we'd try to start the milk flowing.

The first few months, before they started showing, were difficult for us, there was a period of morning sickness, which fortunately didn't last to long. It was also hard that we couldn't tell anyone the good news, like ordinary couples, I mean who can you tell that you, your mother and sister were going to have a baby? Still, the only ones who mattered already knew. When they finally started to show was the happiest time of our lives, we now had physical proof of our love for each other, I mean, knowing they were pregnant was one thing. Actually seeing their stomachs begin to bulge with new life was something else entirely.

Fortunately school was almost over, so Debbie didn't really have any problem hiding her pregnancy. Our final school dance was special, as usual I took Debbie, not that I wanted to take anyone else. We danced all night, every chance we got I held her close, feeling her body against mine, feeling the little bulge of her belly pressing against me. "God, Wayne," Debbie whispered to me during one of our dances, "if only everyone knew you're dancing with your pregnant sister, and you're the one who put my baby in my belly."

"I know. I'm so proud that you and mom are pregnant, I want to tell the world."

"I do too, but it would destroy us. It's been hell since we started making love. Listening to all the other girls talking about their boyfriends, and not being able to talk about mine, because he's also my brother. I've been so happy since you took my virginity, I love you, and mom so much."

I quickly reached down and stroked her belly. "I know you do, Debbie. I can feel the proof right now."

Debbie moved her hips against mine, pushing against my erection, "So can I, Wayne, so can I." She said with a smile. We had a wonderful time when we got home that night, mom had already gone to bed, this night was just for us. I took Debbie out back and we made love under the stars. It was magic.

As their stomachs grew so did my attraction to them. When we were making love I'd always find myself stroking their bellies, in a way, reminding myself that they were carrying my child. And I wasn't the only one. Many times when Debbie and mom were eating each other one or the other would do the same thing, they were just as turned on as I was about making love to a pregnant woman. I loved watching them around the house, with their every growing bellies. Seeing my mother and sister, naked, and obviously pregnant was one thing, knowing that they were carrying my child in their bellies was another. I was almost constantly hard. Fortunately for me they were also almost constantly horny, so it worked out in the end.

I really enjoyed our sunbathing sessions now. Coating them in oil, especially their stomachs, I usually spent as much time, lightly, caressingly, applying the oil to their bellies as the rest of their bodies. But then again so did they. And the end result! They looked magnificent glistening in the sunlight; in fact I took many photos of them by the pool for our ever-growing collection.

Every chance I got my hands went to their stomachs, a favourite time was when we watched TV. I'd sit in the middle and caress their bellies while we watched. Our showers were also fun. Fortunately there was a large shower in moms, or should I say, our bathroom, it had to be, with three people, two of them pregnant. I usually managed to wash their bellies, but even when we were washing ourselves I usually had at least one stomach pressing against me.

As time passed I was no longer able to enter them from the front, so we moved on to other positions. Often I'd take them with us lying on our sides, but our favourite was the doggy position. Here as I slowly worked in and out I was always able to caress their stomachs, once I had them side-by-side on the bed. It was such a sexy sight, mom and Debbie, on their hands and knees, legs spread for my entrance, their stomachs touching the bed, I can't figure out why some men don't think pregnant women are sexy. Is there anything better than having sex with a pregnant woman, with knowing that the woman you are pleasuring, and who is pleasuring you, is fulfilling natures prime directive, increasing the species. That the body you have entered is growing and sheltering a new life, and, that when you touch her stomach you are also touching that life. That the woman you are having sex with loves you enough to have your child, even if, in this case she is your mother or sister.

Then, just when we thought it couldn't get any better, it did, their milk came in. We'd been stimulating their nipples from quite early on, and finally it had worked. At first we got the pre milk, but then the milk proper started to flow, and flow, and flow.

Mom's milk had come in first, that night she got to breast feed her children again, this time we got more out of it than sustenance, we got real pleasure. I had been unsure about how much I'd enjoy the breast milk, I needn't have worried, I loved it. I lay there, moms nipple lightly clasped between my lips, suckling as I had as a baby. I looked across to moms other breast, at Debbie, who was obviously enjoying the experience as much as I was. It must have been quite a sight, a mother, lying naked on her bed, breast-feeding her naked, 18-year-old children. And everyone loved every minute of it. In a way it was even more personal than having sex, mom was feeding us with her own milk, with the milk her body produced. She caressed our heads as we fed, moaning, as she moved to orgasm. Debbie and I kept sucking as she came.

When we finally finished I told mom how much I'd loved her milk, Debbie agreed, saying that she couldn't wait until her milk was in so we could drink hers as well. Mom just smiled, "Me neither."

Debbies milk didn't come in for another 2 weeks. Before that we set up a regular routine with mom. We didn't drink her milk during sex; we kept it a separate activity. When we woke up we had our first meal, draining her breasts before we even got out of bed. Then we'd shower and have our solid breakfast. Since school had finished we went to have lunch with mom at work, everyone thought it great that we were so close. They didn't know that there was no food in the bags we brought with us, that behind moms locked office door her children were drinking her milk. Imagine their reaction if they could see us, mom, sitting in her chair, blouse unbuttoned, nursing bra open, her son, kneeling on one side, suckling at one breast, her pregnant daughter kneeling on the other suckling the other. Then at night she'd feed us before we went to bed. Once in bed we would make love and go to sleep. (I'd make love to Debbie during the day when mom was at work.)

Then Debbies milk arrived. After we'd drained moms breasts Debbie took her place and guided mom and I to her nipples. We latched on and started feeding; her milk was as delicious as moms. There we were, a brother drinking his sisters' milk, milk she had because she was carrying his baby. And a mother drinking her daughters' milk, just as the daughter had hers only moments before. Debbie loved every minute of it, she came just like mom.

So now we had four breasts to drain, since I was draining 2 breasts I drank a lot more milk than the others, I loved it, but I knew I would be cut back when the babies arrived and they would join in the feeding, so I made the most of it. So did the others, they both loved drinking each others milk.

We added Debbie to our routine, the only difference being our draining her milk as well as moms. In the office when we finished with mom, Deb would take her place and we'd suckle her as well.

During the weekend of course all bets were off. It was more catch as catch can, we'd simply take a nipple and start sucking. Once, when I came home after going into town to buy something or another, I found mom and Debbie positioned so that they could drink each others milk at the same time. Deb was on her back and mom was on her knees by her head. They'd decided they couldn't wait to take turns.

Of course we were affected by the start of college. We could no longer take our 'lunch breaks' together. Now mom and Debbie had to express their milk during lunch and bring it home that night. It turned out we preferred our milk direct from the source, still warm. Since we didn't want to waste the milk we experimented and found out that we could use it in our regular food. The taste was slightly different, but we now used breast milk to replace the cows milk in our various meals, pancakes, cakes, scrambled eggs, even mashed potatoes. After all waste not want not.

Wanting to find out how long we could continue drinking their milk we investigated. From our reading we discovered that a woman could continue to produce milk as long as there is a suitable stimulus, she doesn't have to be pregnant. Since the problems of milk production, leaking nipples etc didn't affect me I left it up to mom and Debbie if they wanted to keep producing milk after the babies were weaned. They thought for all of thirty seconds before agreeing that the result was worth the hassles.

All during this time mom and Debbie were moving through their pregnancies. Finally mom went into labour. We rushed her to the hospital and waited through her labour. It took 8 hours, but finally she delivered our daughter, a perfectly healthy baby girl. I was horrified at what mom had gone through, but she said she was surprised how quickly and easily it had happened. Debbie's face turned a little green when she heard that.

When we took them home the baby, Sarah, slipped right into the family. It was a beautiful sight, the first time we watched mom feed our daughter, mom looked so happy and contented, her new daughter suckling at her breast. After the first few days Debbie and I joined in again. Again mom had two of her children at her breast, this time however one was 18 and the other a baby. Often I would feed at one breast while watching Sarah feed at the other, it was wonderful to share the experience with my daughter. Other times mom would feed her two daughters. If Sarah wanted more after moms milk was finished Debbie would offer her breast and Sarah would drink her sisters milk, usually along with her mother.

Then Debbie went into labour. It was a long hard labour, 27 hours in all before; finally, thankfully, Debbie delivered Annie, who was just as healthy as Sarah. In due course they both came home from the hospital and we were complete.

I often fed with both my daughters, though I kept my meals small because I was sharing with mom and Deb, we would rather cut back for a while than run our daughters short. Sometimes mom or Debbie would feed both babies, which provided some quite unusual combinations. Mom would be feeding Sarah, who was both her daughter and granddaughter on one breast, and Annie, who was her granddaughter on both sides of the family on the other. Whereas Debbie would be feeding Annie, who was both her daughter and niece and Sarah, who was her sister and niece. I'm glad I didn't have to try and draw up our family tree.

Finally mom was able to recommence sexual activity, it was something we'd looked forward to, though, having seen what they went through I was a bit reluctant to risk it again, I didn't want to hurt them like that again. They thought I was sweet, but said I was being an idiot. The first time we went extra softly and slow, not wanting to take any chances. It was a bit strange her not being pregnant, both mom and Debbie had really worked at getting back to pre pregnancy condition, they'd both succeeded. Then Debbie was able and we returned to our pre baby activities. Then one day they told me they had something they wanted to talk about.

"Debbie and I have talked it over and decided that we want more children, I want at least one more and Debbie wants another two. But this time we aren't going to do it deliberately. This time its going to be up to nature, we won't go on birth control, but at the same time we won't deliberately try to become pregnant. I've heard that breast-feeding reduces the chance of pregnancy, I don't know if it's true or not. If, in two years I'm not pregnant, I'm going to stop breast-feeding you and Deb, and really try, I don't want a big gap between children, and besides, I don't want to wait too long, the clocks ticking. If that works, once I'm producing milk again, Debbie will stop so she can have her chance. Just think you'll be a father again."

I smiled at the thought, "If that's what you want, its fine with me."

That night as we lay in our bed, our children in the nursery next door. I thought back to how this all started. I realized I'd never complain about bad weather again, in fact I love storms now.

THE END

Share your thoughts with us.
Take a moment to tell us how we're doing. Your feedback really matters.

You can reach us by:
Email: <u>*my777books@yahoo.com*</u>

Search for other titles by **Sophie MacDonald.**